SHOC

MICHAEL ANGELO AVALLONE was born in Manhattan, New York, in 1924. Educated in the Bronx, he served in the United States Army between 1943 and 1946 and returned from the European front a Sergeant. He worked as a stationery salesman from 1946 to 1955 while sharpening his writing skills. He sold his first story 'Aw Let the Kid Hit' to the magazine *Baseball Stories* in 1951 and has never looked back.

He has since written and published over 150 novels and used a multitude of pseudonyms including Edwina Noone, Priscilla Dalton, Dorothea Nile, Jean-Anne de Pre, Dora Highland, Mark Dane, Nick Carter, Steve Michaels, Sidney Stuart, Troy Conway, Vance Stanton, Michele Arlen, Stuart Jason, James Blaine, Max Walker and Lee Davis Willoughby . . .

A veteran of the paperback field, Michael Avallone has written in a whole variety of genres: private eye tales, gothics under his female pseudonyms, juveniles, erotics, espionage, movie and TV tie-in novelisations, and has affectionately been referred to as 'the fastest typewriter East of Pecos'.

His main mystery character is his alter-ego private eye Sam Noon, also a manic movie lover and connoisseur of pneumatic (and cheap) women. Sam Noon has appeared in over 25 novels from *The Spitting Image* (1953) and *The Tall Dolores* (1953) to *High Noon at Midnight* (1938).

Other series characters of Avallone's are April Dancer, Memo Morgan, Satan Sleuth and the Butcher.

Michael Avallone is still writing.

Also available in the Blue Murder series

The Big Clock Kenneth Fearing
Whatever Happened to Baby Jane? Henry Farrell
Solomon's Vineyard Jonathan Latimer
Somebody's Done For David Goodis
Scarface Armitage Trail
The Honeymoon Killers Paul Buck
Texas by the Tail Jim Thompson

Forthcoming

Odds Against Tomorrow William P. McGivern
Straw Dogs Gordon Williams
The Big Enchilada L. A. Morse
Scorpion Reef Charles Williams

Further titles to be announced

Series editor: Maxim Jakubowski

Maxim Jakubowski was born in the UK but educated in France. His first book was published when he was only 19. For many years he juggled his writing with an executive position in the food industry before finally switching to book publishing. He has held senior editorial positions with various British publishing houses. An expert on and lover of science fiction, fantasy and crime fiction, he is also known for his books on film and rock music. Among his over twenty books are *Travelling Towards Epsilon, Twenty Houses of the Zodiac, Lands of Never, Beyond Lands of Never, The Complete Book of SF and Fantasy Lists* (with Malcolm Edwards), *The Rock Yearbook*, two volumes of *The Rock Album, The Great Movies—Live* (with Ron van der Meer) and *The Wit and Wisdom of Rock 'n Roll*. He has contributed to many definitive reference works and has edited two leading crime fiction cult imprints: *Black Box Thrillers* and *Blue Murder*. He lives in London.

SHOCK CORRIDOR

MICHAEL AVALLONE

based on the screenplay by

Samuel Fuller

Xanadu

blue murder

British Library Cataloguing in Publication Data

Avallone, Michael
Shock Corridor.
I. Title
813.54 [F]
ISBN 1-85480-058-2

First published in the USA in 1963 by Belmont Books

First British edition published 1990 in the Blue Murder series by Xanadu Publications Limited, 19 Cornwall Road, London N4 4PH.

Printed and bound in Great Britain by
Cox & Wyman Limited, Reading.

SHOCK CORRIDOR

Author's Note

It is standard operating procedure to precede a work of fiction with the statement *"All persons, places and events in this narrative are entirely fictitious and any resemblance to any person, living or dead, is purely coincidental"*—but one would be hard put to deny the utter reality of Samuel Fuller's masterful screenplay, SHOCK CORRIDOR.

—Michael Avallone
Brooklyn, N. Y.
August 1963

Am I insane?
Guy de Maupassant, Am I Insane?

THE ANTEROOM

"WHEN WAS the first time you got this urge, Mr. Barrett?"

"I'm not sure."

"There must have been a first time, Mr. Barrett."

"When I was fourteen."

"Fourteen, Mr. Barrett?"

"Maybe younger . . . when I was ten. That's when I got the feeling."

"What gave it to you?"

"Her braids."

"Tell me about her braids."

"I got excited."

"Go on."

"I got excited—I said that, didn't I?"

"Yes."

"I grabbed her braids."

"Is that when you hurt her?"

"I'd never hurt her."

"Did you pull on her braids?"

"I caressed them . . . kissed them . . ."

"Did you pull on them?"

"You think I'm a fetishist?"

There was a snort and an explosion of sound in the darkened office. A rising blind flooded the room with sunlight. Johnny Barrett batted his eyes, feeling as red-faced as a schoolboy caught in the weakest lie.

"Hell no, Johnny!" Dr. Fong bellowed in a very un-Oriental show of anger. "Let *them* bring up that word. Not you! You'll be facing the best psychiatrists in the state and they'll know when you're shamming." Disgustedly, he selected a cigar from a chrome humidor on his desk, pierced the tip with a match stick and lit up.

Johnny looked at him fondly, thinking: *I feel sorry for Doc Fong. Professionally he knows he's playing with dynamite but he just couldn't turn down his closest friend.*

Across the room in silent chairs, Swanson sat peeling a tangerine and Cathy was remote, no expression at all on her adorable face. Johnny stemmed a rush of rising anger. No one seemed to think it was a good idea except him. Well, wasn't it always that way?

Swanee and Doc Fong. They were in Psychological Warfare back in War Two. Now the doc was a top-flight head candler and Swanee was Johnny's boss. The editor of the *Daily Globe.* And Cathy was—

"Johnny," Dr. Fong was controlled again, his smooth voice almost professorial. "The role you'll play will be stronger than your strongest imagination, so don't ever weaken. It will be a daily duel between the insane and your own sane mind, and as for the doctors there, lower your mask for an instant and they'll know you're a phony. Never let them forget you're living on a sexual powderkeg. You'll find that Dr. Cristo and his staff will expect you to see a symbol in everything." He held up the cigar. "Remember, it's not always a symbol." He smiled. "Sometimes it's just a cigar." He went back to his desk. "He's all yours, Swanee."

"Think he's ready?" Swanee was still concerned with his tangerine.

"As ready as he ever will be," Dr. Fong concluded.

Swanee nodded, ignored the tangerine and flung a glance across the room. "Well, the next move is yours, Cathy. Johnny's got our blessing."

Johnny had let it all come back to Cathy. As it had to. Everything depended on her cooperation. The three men studied her. She was fixed in her chair, calm, almost statuelike. They had never seen her so pale. Her full lips pulled.

"Caressing my braids. Kissing them," she murmured dully. "What a disgusting story. What happens if they find out I'm not his sister?"

"I'll handle that," Swanee grunted.

Cathy tossed her blonde head, rose from the chair and circled it as if she didn't know where to go. But even in confusion, her body was a symphony, her legs rhapsodic, identifying the professional dancer.

She stared at Johnny, her heart in her eyes.

"You've got to be crazy to want to be committed to an insane asylum to solve a murder that the police gave up on a long time ago."

"Honey," Johnny replied softly, "even if I don't crack the case, my experiences can mean a book, a play, a movie sale. Every man wants to get to the top in his profession. My goal is winning the Pulitzer Prize. And if this story doesn't win me one, nothing ever will."

"Their sickness is bound to rub off on you," Cathy implored desperately.

"That's what I said when you started to sing in your skin for a living. Remember, Cathy? But those hookers didn't knock down your guard and change you, did they? The lunatics won't damage me, either."

Swanee coughed. "Reporters have impersonated coal miners, school teachers, hoodlums. Even bearded ladies—"

"Those reporters," Cathy flared, "went in for a purpose, not to win a journalistic halo on the cover of *Life*, not to win a cash prize and get their pictures in *Time* and *Newsweek*."

Johnny stiffened under the rebuke. "All you have to do is play your part, Cathy."

She caught herself on a sob.

"I'm fed up playing Greek chorus to your rehearsed nightmare. Why don't you smuggle aboard a rocket and write the memoirs of an astronaut? Why don't you forget this psychoanalytical binge?"

Johnny tried to smile. "It's what people buy."

Cathy sucked in her stomach, her breasts rising. Dr. Fong and Swanee exchanged glances. Fong shook his head. They had to stay out of this part of it.

Cathy snorted. "Mark Twain didn't psychoanalyze Huck Finn or Tom Sawyer. Dickens didn't put Oliver Twist on the couch because he was hungry. Good copy comes out of people, Johnny, not out of a lot of explanatory medical terms. You're in a hopped-up, show-off stage. Get off it. Don't be Moses leading your lunatics to the Pulitzer Prize." Her fine figure shivered with revulsion. "I get sick at the thought of you playing games with your mind and riding that crazy horse."

Swanee erupted now. "He's been conditioned for one whole year to ride that horse."

Johnny nodded. "And you've got to saddle it to get me off and running, Cathy."

She shook her long hair. "Scratch me in this race, Johnny."

He rose from the couch, angrily. "We made a deal!"

Her eyes were hard. "My whole instinct is to kick myself hard for ever having gone into this nightmare with you. What I should do is land a righteous punch on your supercivilized nose."

"Cathy, you're an intellectual well past the age of—"

"Don't you dare analyze me!" She looked at him steadily. "Johnny—I'm in love with a normal reporter holding down a normal job. You think I like singing in a sewer with a hot light on my navel? I'm doing it because it pays more than clerking or typing in an office. I'm saving money so that we can *have* that normal life! That's all I want. But I'm scared. I'm scared when I see how calm Dr. Fong and

Swanee and you can be about this crazy scheme of yours. I'm scared this Jekyll-Hyde idea is going to backfire and make a psycho out of *me.*"

Johnny was torn. She needed comforting but he couldn't weaken now. Not with the plan so close to fulfillment. He looked at the faraway wall where Dr. Fong's diplomas were lined up like so much wallpaper.

"You've got to go through with your part, Cathy. There's nobody else I can trust."

"Thank God!"

Johnny's eyes swung back to the contempt in her tone.

"Then go back to your dive!"

"That dive is holy compared to your ideas of work! Hamlet was made for Freud. Not you!"

Johnny Barrett had no suitable answer as Cathy gathered up her things and stormed from the office. The door throbbed like a bull fiddle long after she had gone. Dr. Fong and Swanee waited patiently, watching Johnny's reaction. They both knew how he felt about Cathy. They also knew how he felt about his plan. He had talked of nothing else for weeks.

"My God," Johnny Barrett swore. "She's got to go through with it. We can't swing it without her. Now, isn't that always the way it is with a woman? Just when you need them the most—" His good-looking face was furious as he fumbled for a cigarette.

Dr. Fong's face was Orientally inscrutable this time.

Swanee had returned to his tangerine, peeling with slow, expert fingers.

It took four days for Cathy to make up her mind.

Four days of tortured thinking, nagging doubts that eroded her determination and—four nights of frenzied stripping in the night club where the job "pays more than clerking or typing in an office."

Girls Girls Girls in Pink Flesh and Hot Fantasy

That's what the come-on sign for the suckers always said. In fair or stormy weather. Underneath the gaudy promise of the sign was the popular message: *Featuring Cathy the Singing Stripper*. Underneath that was a king-size glossy photo of the fantastically beautiful Cathy herself. Five feet eight of unimpeachable, unbelievable, nearly naked female perfection.

Inside the noisy, smoke-filled club, the bawdy vicious circle spun nightly. Show after show, with the baby spot following her bared beauty. And the cigars, the looks and the mental rapes.

Cathy, wearing long black gloves that reached above her dimpled elbows. Behind her, a full-length mirror tilted to capture every nuance, every reverse bit of English she put on what Mother Nature had given her.

The blackened backdrop of the stage was a

mass of playing cards, all of the hearts suit. Red hearts to match the pagan atmosphere of the warm thoughts circulating when Cathy sang and stripped.

This wasn't the Cathy that Johnny Barrett loved.

Words of mature concern and adult argument regarding Johnny's plan couldn't have come from this naked salesgirl. The most kissable mouth ever seen in a hot spotlight could not have said the things that Cathy said in Dr. Fong's office. Love? Freud? Don't make me laugh, Buster. I'm shaking my delicious rump in your face.

Cathy slowly stripped as she sang a meaningless song, whose rhythms were more important than the verse. She was feline. With sensuous voice, sensuous personality and more importantly for night club needs, sensuous body. She was offering a song full of Sex.

Her gown fell. The customers gasped inwardly, then audibly.

Cathy's tawny body, decorated with decals of grasping hands. The customers applaud frantically. The long, golden waterfall of Cathy's hair trails down her golden body.

Cathy was tired. Her mind was a riot of worry and grief. But nobody seeing her wriggling and squirming her nudity to burlesque immortality would ever have guessed it those four nights that Johnny Barrett was missing.

She closed her eyes and raised herself on the balls of her feet. She arched her body backward. Her rounded breasts sprang erect as if given sudden life. Her thighs tensed, exposing new curves, more rounded fantasies for the male eye. The dark club throbbed with passion.

Johnny, Johnny, where are you?

The music moved on slowly, rhythmically, timed to the incredible convolutions of the woman that Johnny Barrett loved.

Cathy stripped and sang and tried not to go out of her mind. Her tiger figure, more cat than woman, existed as a mechanical thing set far apart and above the trouble that brewed in her soul.

The customers thumped their hands noisily, yelling for more.

Cathy phoned Johnny on the eve of the fifth day.

"*Daily Globe*," the operator sing-songed.

"Johnny Barrett, please."

"Night off." The sing-song didn't change a beat.

"Mr. Swanson," Cathy said defeatedly.

"City Desk," Swanee said gruffly when the call was switched to his busy line.

"Swanee—" She fought back the tears. "It's been four whole days, Swanee—"

"You called the shot," he said unkindly.

"*I haven't heard from him in four days*. Is that fair?"

"If you love him," Swanee said impersonally into the phone, "you'd go the limit for him."

That was all to be said.

Cathy hung up, her face dead.

Around her, in the crowded dressing room, the other strippers were getting ready. Their rigged fixtures and breakaway gowns were being readied for their acts. Cathy stared at her own reflection in the dirty mirror. Gaudy, overpainted faces and powdered bodies bobbed and weaved in the glass. Cathy's eyes filled. She was crying. The other girls left her alone, knowing full well the trouble she was having with her newspaper boy friend.

Cathy was too busy with her grief to hear a stripper suddenly shrill in an outraged voice: "Hey, no men in here! Off limits, Junior!"

She only felt Johnny Barrett's strong hands fall on her naked shoulders, lifting her out of the chair. She whirled, seeing him in the mirror first, then melting into his embrace. Blindly, she kissed him, her heart rising high and free. He was back. Johnny was back. Her Johnny. His mouth burned away the sorrow.

"Johnny, Johnny. I'll do it."

"You're sure? No mistake?"

"Yes," she whispered in his ear. "If that's what you want—"

He nodded swiftly, his enthusiastic face alive with her acceptance. "Honey, it is. I'll die if I don't do this thing."

Cathy stared at him, her eyes still swimming.

This was Johnny. Her Johnny. Hustling, hard-working Johnny Barrett who had worked himself up from copyboy to one of the best newspapermen in the city. Maybe the world. How could she say for sure that he wouldn't turn this idea of his into the wonderful thing he wanted it to be.

She couldn't argue with him any more. Four days, the penalty for disagreement, had washed away all her fears and pessimism. She was more afraid of losing Johnny than anything else.

"Johnny, take me home. I want to make love. I want to talk. I want to hold you again. My arms ache for you."

He nodded, smiling.

"Deal. And then we'll make our plans. I want to move this thing right away. No delay."

They worked it out that night.

"What can I do for you, young lady?"

The police lieutenant behind the high desk had been reading a homicide report but at first sight of the tall, long-haired stunner standing before him, he had slipped into the unfamiliar role of extreme courtesy.

"I want to report something." The girl sounded nervous. The lieutenant recognized the opening.

"Sure, lady. Go ahead."

"My brother won't let me alone," Cathy said. "He wants to . . . sleep with me." She had gone over the words a thousand times but she still couldn't believe she had finally said them.

"How old is he?" For her benefit, the lieutenant pretended she hadn't said anything shameful or unusual.

"Thirty."

"Are you married?"

"No."

"Does he live with you?"

"No."

Business like. Official. That made it easier.

"Has he ever attacked you?"

"He's tried."

"Did he ever hurt you?"

"Yes."

The lieutenant nodded. "Have you ever brought charges against his sickness?"

Oh, Lord. She shook her head.

"Why not?"

"I was . . . ashamed."

"And now?"

"He said he'll kill me if I don't . . ." Cathy didn't have to act any more. The lie made her mumble, lower her eyes.

"Are you ready to sign a formal complaint that he's mentally unsound?"

Cathy could only nod.

"That means a police request for a psychopathic examination," the lieutenant was telling her as if she didn't understand.

She nodded again.

"I didn't hear you, Miss."

"Yes."

There was a harsh, rattling noise as the lieutenant placed a sheet of paper into a typewriter.

"What's your brother's full name?"

"John Barrett." *Oh, Lord, Johnny!*

The sounds of typing pierced her hearing like separate, deadly bullets of damnation. The lieutenant spoke into a ready phone.

"County General Hospital? Psycho Unit, please . . ." He turned to Cathy. His eyes showed nothing. "Your name?"

"Cathy." It was a whisper.

"C or K?"

It took a thousand horses to pull the 'C' out of her mouth. The lieutenant typed with one finger, holding onto the phone, speaking into it: "Dr. Menkin? Kane. Sixteenth Precinct."

Cathy could only stare as the lie got under way, gathered a full head of steam and roared on into reality.

"Name of subject: John Barrett. Attempted incest with sister," the lieutenant was saying with factual emphasis, "soon as we pick him up we'll send him over for emergency admission."

Cathy stared down at the floor of the police station. It was dirty; splattered and scuffed with the residue of thousands of soles and heels. She shivered involuntarily.

All around her, the nightmare revolved.

"You've got no right jackassing me down here on her say-so," Johnny Barrett roared in the confines of Dr. Menkin's office. "I'm a reporter on the *Globe*! Call my boss. He'll vouch for me, goddammit!"

Dr. Menkin pried open his fingers and spread

them, gesturing to the uniformed policeman standing in the doorway. Cathy was seated in a chair on the other side of the desk, looking at nobody, seeing nothing.

"We've checked with Mr. Swanson," Dr. Menkin said affably. "He gave you a clean bill of health—"

"That's more like it!"

"—but his word doesn't carry much weight since your sister signed a formal complaint against you."

Johnny sneered, "What do you expect from a stripper?" He advanced across the room toward Cathy. "Go on, Sis, tell him you dreamed up the whole thing."

The policeman waited, motionless.

Cathy stared dumbly ahead. Only the policeman's eyes showed his feelings. Cathy could guess what he was thinking though. *Beautiful girl. Too bad it's her brother trying to crawl into bed with her.*

"Please sit down, Mr. Barrett." Dr. Menkin indicated the empty chair across from the desk.

Johnny shrugged, ignored Cathy and sat down. He kept a face of righteous indignation on.

"Is your father alive?" Dr. Menkin asked smoothly.

"No."

"Did you like him?"

"Of course."

"Any brothers?"

"No."

"Any other sisters?" Dr. Menkin pursued.

"Just Cathy," he said feelingly. "That's enough."

"Did you ever want to sleep with her?"

Johnny permitted himself to be shocked. "That's a filthy thing to ask me."

Dr. Menkin was patient. "We're here to help you." There was a short silence. "You love Cathy, don't you?"

"She's my sister."

"You love her as a woman, don't you?" Dr. Menkin was quietly persistent.

Johnny laughed. "You think I'd let some meathead deflower her?"

Dr. Menkin nodded as if he understood. "Mothers and fathers have the same fears."

"You understand me, don't you, Doc?"

"Of course . . . when was the first time you got the urge to make love to your sister?"

Johnny maintained a thoughtful expression. This was the tough part. Pretending to remember.

"There must have been a first time," Menkin said quietly.

"When I was fourteen."

He was gratified at the manner in which the doctor's placid face awoke. *Look at the way his eyes lit up. He's got me talking now and he's a happy little rascal, this Menkin.*

"Fourteen?"

"Maybe younger. When I was ten, say. That's when I got the feeling." Cathy gasped audibly in the stillness of the office. But Johnny didn't hear her. He was focused on Menkin, waiting for the sixty-four-thousand-dollar question.

Now if you ask me what gave it to me, this story will write itself.

"What gave it to you?" Dr. Menkin asked.

"Her braids," Johnny responded promptly.

"Tell me about her braids."

"I got excited."

"Go on."

"I got excited . . . I said that, didn't I?"

"Yes."

"I grabbed her braids."

"And hurt her."

"I'd never hurt her."

"Did you pull on her braids?"

"I caressed them," Johnny said warmly. "I kissed them." The policeman at the door shifted his feet uncomfortably. Cathy kept her eyes on the wall at a point above Dr. Menkin's head.

"Did you pull on them?" the doctor repeated.

"Told you I'd never hurt her, didn't I?"

Dr. Menkin got up from behind the desk, frowning. John watched him, his thought processes still whirling. *The next question's got to be about a fetishist, according to Doc Fong's script.*

"Know what a fetishist is?"

Bullseye. It was easy to laugh. Everything was going good.

"Sure, I know. What about it?"

The doctor had seated himself again. His eyes showed the professional hope that the next question would open all the doors.

"As a reporter, have you ever covered a story where a man became intensely excited sexually whenever he saw a woman with long hair? Long, loose hair?"

"Yes."

"Did he make love to her?"

"Yes. He killed her."

Dr. Menkin looked pleased. "You don't want to wake up one fine morning to learn you killed your sister, do you?"

"No!" Johnny barked heatedly. "And I'm certainly no epileptic with a fetish for hair. Of course, with Cathy, her hair is different."

Menkin nodded. "I understand, Mr. Barrett."

"I figured you would."

"Didn't you threaten to commit suicide if she ever got married? Think now. Didn't you threaten your sister if she didn't let you make love to her?"

"That's different."

"Why?"

"Because *she's* different."

"Why is she different?"

"Because!" Johnny squirmed on his chair.

"Because why?"

Johnny leaped to his feet, exploding, the smile on his face dissolving into white hot rage. "Because I love her, you damn fool! I want her to have my baby and nobody's going to keep us apart!" As if faced with the physical possibility of such an eventuality, Johnny hurled himself across the desk at Dr. Menkin. The policeman at the door roared in his throat and moved fast.

Johnny pummeled the doctor about the shoulders with flying fists, all the while yelling, "Cathy! Cathy! Cathy . . . !" The policeman reached him, dragged him back forcibly from Menkin and locked him in a bear hug. Menkin sagged in his chair, rubbing his shoulders.

It was a great act for Johnny Barrett and Cathy. Dr. Fong and Swanee might have applauded out loud had they been there to witness the ruse.

But Cathy was no longer acting.

She had buried her face in her painted fingers, the tears burning, the sobs making her lithe body shake uncontrollably.

Dr. Menkin made all the tests prescribed by state law and the science of psychoanalysis—Emotional Tendencies and Temperament... Attitude Toward Material Needs... Attitude Toward Oneself... Emotional State... Personality Synthesis... Emotional State...

Dr. Menkin's assistant, loaded down with the batch of reports, was in a talkative mood.

"You ought to see what the strain has done to his sister, Dr. Menkin."

"How long has he been under observation now?"

"A week." The assistant handed over a clipped stack of sheets. "His free-association tests. This Barrett is a lulu—" Through the half-opened door of the office, Cathy patiently waited for Dr. Menkin to call her in. When the voices of Menkin and his assistant filtered out to her and she realized what they were saying, she slipped a notebook out of her purse, found a pencil and took shorthand notes in quick, furtive lines. Only her face revealed her agitation.

Dr. Fong's apartment office was the proper place to bring the shorthand notes. Swanee was on hand too, looking happy with the way things were going and fairly rubbing his hands.

Cathy read her notes aloud, almost tonelessly. "*.....Barrett shows a culmination of an internal sexual conflict which is generally of old standing and based on a constitutionally determined chaotic sexual makeup. There's no doubt his patterns of symptoms in a mental disease is familiar. We've got to resolve the underlying sexual conflict. Whenever he wants his sister physically, he is taking the form of a mental breakdown. An acute schizophrenic episode.*"

She stopped reading and looked at Dr. Fong. "What does it mean?"

Fong twinkled at her. "Means I'm a pretty good teacher and Johnny's a smart student."

"So far, so good," Swanee crowed.

Cathy stamped her foot. "I don't mean that! Aren't either of you concerned about his breakdown?"

Dr. Fong was confused. "What breakdown?"

"Taking all those tests is bound to *make* him sick."

Swanee grunted. "You're right, that *is* something to worry about. If he breaks down they'll trap him and toss him right out on his rump."

"On the contrary," Fong demurred. "I think

he's captured the perfect mood of the borderline psychosis exactly as we rehearsed it. And if the superior court judge buys Johnny's performance, he'll be committed."

"That's great," Cathy wailed to no one in particular. "And I did it all. With my little hatchet—"

Swanee and Dr. Fong let her cry in silence.

In Johnny Barrett's County Hospital room, he had a nightmare. It shouldn't have been a nightmare because it was all about Cathy. But nightmare it was.

He saw her full figure, stripping. There was a dark haze all around with only her white body showing through. Instead of singing, she was speaking. Even as she peeled the garments from her mammoth breasts and long, golden thighs.

"You were a healthy lover until you started this crazy idea, Johnny. It's consumed you and made a nervous wreck out of me . . . Reverse the situation, Johnny. What if *I* were going away on a job that would separate us for weeks or months? Would you help me put a gap between us . . . ?"

He rolled in his sleep, damp body staining the coarse sheets of the cot. Cathy's image shimmered, showed more flesh. Her breasts were rippling.

"The drama critic on your paper said my Chablis-tinted hair was a sensuous halo over soft, inviting wide-set eyes and my generous mouth was a lush tunnel through which golden notes came..."

He groaned in his sleep.

"...and my movements evoked the most inflammatory passions in all male spectators..."

His voice roared soundlessly to stop her. *"Stop it, Cathy!"*

"...Why don't you stop, Johnny...?"

"I miss you, Cathy," he mumbled. "My yen for you goes up and down like a fever chart."

Her breasts danced closer. The red mouth gaped.

"...I don't like being alone, Johnny..."

"I love you, Cathy!" He tried to reach her but her lithe nudeness wavered and floated away. Only her voice and patches of bare, maddening flesh lingered to hurt him.

"...But you've made me be alone, Johnny ...and I have a right to select my own bedfellow..."

"Cathy!" His fingers were molasses, sticking to his body, incapable of catching her.

"Go ahead...pretend to be crazy...catch the man who killed that lunatic...get your scoop, your Pulitzer Prize...but you won't have me...will you?...which do you want more, Johnny...?"

"Cathy! Don't go!"

He awoke to darkness and utter stillness, aware only of having slept poorly. The corridor outside his cell was dim and quiet.

Johnny Barrett trembled.

He was breathing hard, sweating hard, staring hard.

He would have given anything in the world for a cigarette at that precise moment. He smiled ruefully in the shadows of his cell.

He might even have given away his ingenuous scheme to solve the murder of Sloan, the inmate who had been knifed so terribly in the State Mental Hospital.

Sloan, whose murderer was still running around loose.

Sloan, whose murderer had to be someone who lived in the State Mental Hospital.

As a patient, attendant or official... who might kill again.

Delirium is a disease of the night.
Charles Jackson, The Lost Weekend

THE CORRIDOR

WILKES, the attendant, was Johnny Barrett's first real acquaintance with State Mental Hospital. He'd seen prisons and jailhouses and asylums before, so high grey walls and cell-blocks and long corridors were pretty much the same. The place had no personality for him yet. Only Wilkes did. Wilkes was genial and talkative. Johnny decided he liked him as the man led him toward his ward.

Johnny was already in the uniform of an inmate. Grey denim shirt with matching pants. The material was coarse and scratchy. Wilkes' badge of authority seemed to be the standard uniform of attendants. White shirt, black bow tie, white pants, white shoes. A whistle looped on a cord dangled from his neck. From his pocket, attached to his belt, a long key chain glistened. Wilkes' had Johnny's record papers under his arm and had been vocally impressed with them.

"140 I.Q. classification. Very good, Mr. Barrett. Means superior intelligence. Sometimes a fooler but we'll see. Tomorrow Dr. Cristo will decide the best therapy for you." For all the world, he might have been a social instructor at a Catskill resort.

"The shower was good but why did I have to have another physical? I had one at County Hospital."

Wilkes smiled. "Regulations. You know." He confided suddenly, "We've got a 170 man here."

"Dr. Cristo?"

"No, a patient."

Johnny thought fast. There had been three inmates who'd witnessed the murder he had to crack. An ex-GI, a Negro student and a Nobel Prize winning physicist, Dr. Boden. Two to one, the man with the 170 I. Q. was Boden.

"One-seventy? That's near genius, isn't it?"

"That *is* genius," Wilkes affirmed.

"And you say he's a patient?"

"We get all kinds up here, Mr. Barrett," Wilkes concluded sadly. Johnny hiked up his pants. Wilkes grinned again.

"You'll have to get used to no belt, no suspenders, no shoelaces."

"I never did like a belt."

"That's the attitude to take."

They had reached a screen door somewhere in the maze of hallway. Wilkes halted Johnny before another attendant. The man's white outfit contrasted sharply with a beetle-browed face and skeptical eyes.

"New patient, Lloyd. John Barrett."

Lloyd checked an assignment book propped over his forearm.

"Ward B. Bed Two." He unlocked the screen door and flung a glance at Johnny. "Barrett, eh?"

Johnny tensed. Lloyd's attitude was unfriendly, suspicious; like so many people he'd interviewed down through the reportorial years. He sensed belligerence and got ready for it.

"So you're the 140 I.Q. journalist, eh? Where's your typewriter?"

"Easy, Lloyd," Wilkes said warningly.

Lloyd made a face. "The last reporter I had on this floor was Ben Franklin and that egghead gave me more trouble than—"

Wilkes stepped between them. "Come on, Mr. Barrett."

"Born phonies, all you newspapermen," Lloyd continued, staring at Johnny. Johnny looked past him. Inside his head, a warning sign went up: *This knothead Lloyd I've got to watch.*

The room behind the screen door was a long corridor.

There was a ceiling strip of light that seemed to run into infinity. Johnny was aware of a peculiar hum of sound that was like no other sound he had ever heard. Wilkes, at his elbow, coughed, "You came at the make-friends hour."

That was puzzling, somehow. Johnny found himself staring at the scene before him. Some of the patients were in tiny groups, others were sitting on the drab benches; still others were seated on the floor, legs crossed like so many Hindus in the marketplace. The sight was unnerving. Each of the men and the tiny groups, meaningless expanses of grey denim, gave off the barely discernible hum of sound that was so hard to identify.

"Patients who behave," Wilkes was explaining with long familiarity with the words, "are permitted to congregate in this corridor—they call it 'The Street.' Gives them a chance to make new friends. The women have their street too. I used to work in the female wing but the nympho ward got too dangerous for me."

Johnny was barely listening. The faces before him were exactly as Dr. Fong had described them. All the faces had born witness to his entrance among them. Tragic faces, false faces, smiling faces. Some curious, some without expression of any nature. Some of the faces challenged Johnny. As if daring him to make a comment. Johnny mentally catalogued the facts as Doc Fong had outlined them: *mute catatonics . . . quietly depressed manic-depressives . . . excitable manic-depressives . . . paranoid schizophrenics . . . tractable schizophrenics . . . borderline homicidal maniacs . . . hysterial paralysis.*

And me. Johnny Barrett, hebephrenic schizophrenic suffering from sexual hallucinations and emotional deterioration . . . oh, Cathy, what a story this is going to make.

Wilkes led Johnny among them. The effect was electric. Some of the men hid their faces, others glared. A few slunk away to other corners of the corridor. And still the hum and pitch of their low voices ran on like some low-playing radio. Johnny held back a feeling of fear and revulsion. The pity within him was having a difficult time staying on top.

What are they hiding from, these God-haunted ghosts? he thought.

The mocking line stayed with him all the way to his ward as Wilkes guided him. *That's not bad for a lead... "God-haunted ghosts, bereft of reason, living in shadows, in the long corridor of delusion, their lost faculties suspended in the gallery of the grotesque..." No, too flowery. Swanee would slug that kind of copy 'molasses.' Shakespeare ought to be with me right now. What did he have Hamlet say? Oh, yes... "Though this be madness, yet there is method in it"... Method? What method? They're not of this planet... not these men.*

"Here we are," Wilkes said.

Ward B was a door with a small window in the frame. When Wilkes pushed the door in, Johnny saw a deserted ward with six beds, three to either side of a narrow room. Wilkes pointed to the one nearest the door.

"This one is yours."

"Am I the only loony in this ward?"

"No, Mr. Barrett. Your roommates are in The Street. If you don't mind, we never use words like nuts, bugs, screwy, goofy, loony. We'd like it if you didn't use them either."

Johnny could see he meant the reproof only as kindness.

"Sorry. I'm a greenhorn inmate."

"You are a patient, not an inmate."

Johnny shrugged. "This is an asylum, isn't it?"

Wilkes smiled. "This is a mental hospital and

we are dealing with mental hygiene. After Dr. Cristo takes you in hand, you'll be a different man. Dr. Cristo's staff has one of the best records in the country."

"I really don't belong here," Johnny blurted.

"I understand." Wilkes' face was always kind. "But you won't cause any trouble, will you? As you did when you attacked the County Hospital psychiatrist?"

"I forgot myself."

"We're here to help you remember not to forget."

Johnny nodded. "May I phone my sister?"

"No. I'm sorry."

"I'm hungry," Johnny said suddenly.

"Lloyd will show you your place in the dining room." He saw the wince on Johnny's face. "What's the matter?"

"Is Lloyd the keeper that called me a phony?"

"He's no keeper," Wilkes said patiently. "He's an attendant like me."

Johnny let his voice fall into a monotone.

"Lloyd doesn't like me."

"Don't mind him," Wilkes said, fatherly. "He doesn't mean anything by his chip on the shoulder. Just his way of fighting everybody because he can't cure the patients."

With that, Wilkes waved and left. Johnny went over to the bed that was his from now on and sat down to think. There was an awful lot to put together before he began making like a detective. He hardly realized how he had fallen into the habit of talking to himself all the time now. It was as if he had to carry on a conversation with a hidden stranger. The real Johnny Barrett who was not pretending to be crazy.

Well, you made it, Johnny. You're in. Now let's recap: A patient named Sloan was murdered in this bughouse. In the kitchen. With a butcher knife. Fingerprints were rubbed off. That means a sane man—an employee. But a lunatic in a sane moment could have wiped off his fingerprints, too.

Johnny stared at the three wire mesh windows that let some daylight into Ward B.

Wonder who's in the bed next to mine? Maybe he's the one who killed Sloan. Wouldn't that be an O. Henry twist? Sleeping next to my story.

He stopped thinking out loud, his thoughts racing. O. Henry never lived this kind of a story. Neither did de Maupassant. Poor Cathy. Trying to back out at the last minute with a woman's fears and a woman's talk. Took imagination to think of a plan like this, didn't it? Cathy couldn't realize what an explosion the yarn was going to make if its possibilities ever paid off. Cathy. Johnny pushed memories of her smooth loveliness out of his mind.

Ward B was silent. Johnny jumped up and paced the room, waiting for his fellow occupants to put in an appearance. The imp behind his eyes went to work on him again.

Ever since my voice changed I've wanted to be in the company of the newspaper greats. And this corridor is the magic highway to the Pulitzer Prize.

He had gone back through the door and was

staring down the corridor at the massed group of inmates.

Maybe I'm looking at the killer right now.

The faces of the men told him nothing. They each were grey, indistinct, part of a common mass. Johnny curbed his restlessness and tried to piece the thing out again in his mind.

Three patients had been found with the dead Sloan, according to all the printed accounts in the *Globe* file. Individually, each man had admitted the crime and then accused each other. One of them had even claimed he *was* Sloan. Then they all had sworn that Sloan never existed. What could the police do but throw out the testimony and admit that an unsolved case was alive and kicking? What did it matter as long as the killer, one of the three men, was safely behind the walls of an institution?

Was Sloan's killer pathological or sane? Why should a harmless little loony like Sloan be killed? Even the police couldn't find a proper motive. For all of Dr. Fong's coaching, Johnny could answer none of these questions.

A tall doctor in white moved down the hall, past Johnny's door.

Good thing we didn't let the doctors here in on my masquerade. One of them might be the killer. Maybe the doc who just passed me. Doc Fong says nobody knows when a lunatic gets a lucid moment. My job's to live with one around the clock and be there when he's sane for a flash.

There were three witnesses, all right.

Stuart, Trent and Boden. Any one or all three had killed Sloan. An ex-GI, a Negro student and a Nobel Prize physicist. There was a list of suspects for you!

Johnny didn't realize he was back sitting on his bed until the door to Ward B swung inward. A mountain of a man gazed silently at him from the threshold, filling the entrance. The man was immense with wide shoulders and spreading girth that tented down from his small head.

"How do you do?" the man rumbled in a big voice. "I am Pagliacci."

"Johnny Barrett." Their hands met and Pagliacci's five fingers were a vise of strength.

"Welcome to Ward B."

Pagliacci said no more and moved across the room and sprawled on his bed. He swept up a battered magazine and began reading. It was as if Johnny was no longer in the room. The bed didn't collapse as Johnny expected it to. He had just identified the magazine as a musical publication when the door opened again. A second patient had shuffled in. He seemed all of seventy. Saying nothing, he went to one corner of the room, ignoring his bed and squatted, pulling a sweater over his leathery face. A third patient wandered in lifelessly and flopped on his bed before Johnny could form a mental picture of him. Two more men entered quickly, sat at the tiny wooden table in the center of the room and began to play a game of cards without comment. They were both nondescript and grey.

Johnny looked up to see the big man watching him with open amusement in his fat face.

"If you expect a demonstration of insanity,

forget it," Pagliacci warned. "The old one there, we call him Methuselah. His mother committed him when he was ten. This hospital was a shack then. He hasn't spoken to anyone for sixty years. The card players are Jekyll and Hyde, the split-personality twins. The one on the bed is suffering from unrelieved melancholy. What are you in for?"

Johnny Barrett could only stare at all of them and fight back against a sudden rush of overwhelming dread, washing over his insides.

"They tell me I'm in love with my sister," he lied.

"That's nice," Pagliacci said, rolling over and returning to his music magazine.

The dining room was another acid test.

The grey, shuffling inmates were allowed to sit four at a table. Johnny stood on a long line which selected trays and filed past a serving counter. Steam filled the room. The faces of the patients were all mute and unmoving. It was an eerie sensation; as if everyone had made a tacit agreement not to talk in line.

Food, in huge silver platters and vats, was carried out from the hidden kitchen to the serving counter.

Lloyd, the disagreeable attendant, materialized at Johnny's elbow when he left the line with a tray of food.

"This is your place from now on, Winchell. Pick yourself a chair." He indicated the table.

"Thank you," Johnny said, forcing himself to be polite.

"Just behave yourself and we'll work out fine."

The table turned out to be shared by Pagliacci, Methusaleh and Jekyll and Hyde. Unrelieved Melancholy was off somewhere else. Johnny forgot his meal and scrutinized the other tables.

He restrained a visible start when he spied Stuart at the table just behind him. Witness Number One. Ollie Stuart. The man was bent over his tray but he wasn't eating. Johnny craned his neck and recognized the colored war map spread out before Stuart. *Gettysburg* in red block letters was apparent even from this distance. It all fit.

Farm boy from the Bible Belt. GI in Korea. Captured, brainwashed, defected to the Commies, dishonorably discharged. Hobby—playing Civil War games. Believes he is General Jeb Stuart, confederate hero of the Civil War.

"Eat," Pagliacci rumbled. "You can see all you want later. You'll have all the time there is."

Johnny returned to the stew on his tray, the paper cup on the table and the cardboard spoon. He picked it up and bent it slowly.

"No knives or forks allowed," Pagliacci explained. "They think we might hurt ourselves."

All about their table the other patients were eating. One man was spoon feeding another catatonic as though he were a child. Another was attacking his stew with all the fervor of a hog. Johnny shuddered at the sight. Men were either staring at their food or wolfing it ravenously.

His eyes came back to Pagliacci, Methuselah, Jekyll and Hyde. They looked annoyed with him.

Johnny lowered his eyes and tried to feign interest in his meal.

Sleep wasn't easy his first night in Ward B. Ponderous snoring buffeted the walls of the room. Johnny tossed on his cot, eyes open, watching the huddled bodies of his wardmates in their respective beds. A little moonlight trickled through the three wire mesh windows. The hospital was dry and seemingly airless.

The snoring was permeated by a peculiar sound. Johnny strained to identify the noise. With a start, he realized that someone was *chewing*. Alert, he hunched forward in his cot.

There was no need to search. Pagliacci was sitting up in bed, staring at him, his puffy cheeks busy with some morsel. Before Johnny could speak, the big man held out something to him.

"Have a stick of gum." His voice was a bull frog in the darkness.

Johnny took it and began to chew.

Pagliacci nodded approvingly and extended more sticks from beneath his pillow.

"Have another. Here. Chew the whole pack."

Under Pagliacci's compelling manner, Johnny found himself chewing five slices of gum like an automaton.

"Pretty soon your jaw muscles will get tired and then the other muscles get the message and *they* get tired and next thing you know, you're asleep. That's how I licked my insomnia. And when we're asleep nobody can tell a sane man from an insane man. Goodnight, Mr. Barrett."

"Goodnight, Mr. Pagliacci."

The remedy worked.

Johnny chewed industriously until the spearmint flavor of the gum was only a pleasant memory. The room darkened. His jaws slowed. The fever pitch of the day stilled his waking brain. A heavy sleep closed over him. A sleep invaded by haunting dreams of Cathy again. Cathy dancing, Cathy reaching for him, Cathy going away. Cathy saying, *"All the men want me, Johnny, and I want you but you want the Pulitzer Prize."*

Then Cathy started singing.

But it didn't sound like Cathy.

Johnny frowned in his sleep, poised between semi-consciousness and awareness.

"Tu se' Pagliaccio!"

Italian. Cathy didn't know any Italian—

Johnny sat up in bed like a jack-in-the-box, his eyes flying open, all of his nerve ends chilled.

The room was dark, the other patients were still asleep but Pagliacci was awake. Pagliacci, standing on some unseen stage between the beds, alternately sobbing and laughing, hands pressed to his chest in the classic posture of Caruso.

"Il nome! Il nome!" Pagliacci's mighty voice bellowed but Methuselah, Jekyll and Hyde and Unrelieved Melancholy slept on. Only Johnny Barrett was a frightened witness.

He could see the big man's wild eyes strain to hear the silent chorus of *"No! Santo diavolo! Fa daverro . . ."*

But Pagliacci had suddenly sprung forward with all the agility of a cat, landed on Johnny's stomach and pinned him down, his long arms encircling. Johnny was speechless with amazement. Pagliacci's grasp was amazingly deft, though his immense weight made it impossible for Johnny to move. He made a stabbing motion with his right hand.

Pagliacci raised his right hand as if it contained a knife.

He quested with his eyes, straining again for the chorus of *I Pagliacci* which would trigger the responses in his mad brain. Even Johnny thought he could hear the words . . . *"Ferma! A te! Que fai! Di morte negli spasimo lo dirai!"* Pagliacci stabbed Johnny again.

Pagliacci's sweaty face glistened.

"Soccorso . . . Silvio! Nedda!"

Johnny saw the gleam in Pagliacci's eyes. His jowls quivered and his lips parted in answer: *"Ah! Sei tu? Ben venga!"* With that, he plunged his imaginary dagger into Johnny's heart again.

Pagliacci removed himself from Johnny's chest and stood up, swaying. He cocked his head, picking up some more messages from the invisible chorus. Johnny held his breath, thunderstruck. He couldn't move. It was a nightmare come to life.

Pagliacci drew himself proudly to his great height, his whole being shattered but his eyes glowing like coals in the darkness. He looked at the dagger in his hand, spread his fingers and watched it fall.

"La commedia e finita!" he boomed melodiously.

The tragedy of Pagliacci was over, with its pointedly ironic last line. The big man was bowing from the waist grandly. Johnny found his hands coming together in weak applause.

But the comedy had not yet ended. There was nothing funny about the utter absorption consuming the big man as he leveled his eyes at Johnny Barrett.

"Thank you," he said humbly. "It was in the middle of that aria that I pitched forward on my face—like this." He allowed himself to crash to the floor. He did that deftly, too. From the floor, he sighed loudly. "—and died of a heart attack caused by overweight."

He pretended to find the invisible dagger and pick it up, hefting it in one fat paw. Johnny stared, refusing to believe that the others could sleep through all this noise.

"A knife is a messy weapon, Mr. Barrett. It was a knife that killed Sloan in the kitchen."

Johnny Barrett stilled the flash of triumph bubbling on his lips. Pagliacci flung the knife into the far wall as he stood up. Then he brushed off his hands.

"The reason so many people showed up at

my funeral was because they wanted to be sure I was dead."

He sat on the edge of Johnny's bed, staring mutely across the room. Johnny found his voice.

"Do you know who used the knife on Sloan?"

Pagliacci had not heard him. He was lost in some dream world of his own making.

"I took my time killing my wife." He leaned toward Johnny. "Did you know that a patient here named Sloan was killed in the kitchen with a butcher knife? It's still an unsolved murder. I despise butchery. I didn't want my wife to die like Sloan so I gently sang her to death. And now, half shrouded in the midst of the great arias in *Carmen, Don Giovanni, I Pagliacci, La Boheme*—I miss her." A great sob racked his big body. "Do you miss her?"

"Yes," Johnny said.

Pagliacci reached out, grabbed his hand.

"The distance between husband and wife is interesting, isn't it?"

Before Johnny could whip up an answer that might have satisfied the giant, Pagliacci had sighed ponderously and gone back to his own bed. He sprawled, face down, sobbing mightily into his pillow. Johnny watched from his own cot, baffled.

There was one wonderful thing about the horror that had just been enacted.

Pagliacci had remembered the murder of Sloan. Which meant that lunatics do have flashes of sanity. They do have total recall of isolated happenings.

Johnny made up his mind he would just have

to be on deck when those flashes of lightning illuminated the dark mentalities of Stuart, Trent and Boden.

He finally slept, lulled by the sobs of Pagliacci, the snoring from one of the beds in the corner and the waltzing tumble of all the colliding images and ideas at war in his tired brain.

For once, Cathy's tormenting face and figure let him be.

—and then some idiot turned on the lights.
Ray Bradbury, The October Game

THE DOOR

DR. CRISTO'S OFFICE was a surprisingly sunny place. Not even the grim portraits of Freud, Jung and Adler could mar the pleasant atmosphere. Morning sunshine bathed the place with warm colors, thanks to a wide window facing south.

Johnny Barrett waited in the chair across from Dr. Cristo's desk. The psychiatrist was studying Johnny's papers and records, going carefully over each page, his unlined face lean and attractive. The man seemed fortyish and alert. Johnny prepared himself for a grueling test. Cristo might not be so easy to fool.

Without looking up, Cristo said, "When I was a young pup, I wanted to be a reporter. A star reporter. Write the big scoop—expose the killer and—marry the publisher's daughter." He folded the sheets, dropped them with finality on his desk top and looked at Johnny.

"You started in as a copy boy, I see."

"When I was fourteen."

"And supported your sister."

"Yes." Johnny braced himself inwardly. *Here it comes again.*

"Did you sleep well?" Dr. Christo purred smoothly.

Johnny whistled a few notes from *Pagliacci.* "I'm an opera lover, Doctor."

Cristo smiled. "Pagliacci is harmless. Barrett, I want to help you but I need your cooperation."

"I understand."

"Why didn't you cooperate with my staff this morning?"

"They want to hurt me."

"Do *I* want to hurt you?"

"Oh," Johnny said offhandedly, "I've been watching you every minute since I've been here."

"Do you know who I am?"

"Of course."

"Who am I?"

Johnny's inner voice went to work: *Dr. Cristo, Clinical Director and head of the medical staff here for seven years. Married, two children. Hobby: golf, sometimes skiing at Sun Valley. Wrote two books on schizophrenia. Yankee fan.*

Aloud, he said, "Don't you know?"

Dr. Cristo's expression changed. Johnny had put on a blank look that indicated his mind was miles away. But he knew what was coming, was ready for it.

"Do you hear voices?"

"Yes. My head hurts. You've got to let me

out of here. Call my paper. They can't go to press unless I'm there. Is Cathy all right?"

"That's why you're here, John." The doctor was trying all the tricks of his trade now. Sudden familiarity. "To make sure that she *will* be all right. Do you understand?"

Johnny made a show of anger. "Why did you have to fingerprint me? I committed no crime."

"You are not in prison, John," Dr. Cristo said gently.

"He told me I shouldn't love her as a woman." Johnny fed him the *non sequitur* line deliberately.

"Who told you?"

"The man on TV. He looked right at me and told me it was naughty. How would he know? He never met Cathy."

Cristo's interest was apparent in his eyes. "Does he talk to you often?"

"Whenever I turn on TV."

"Could the man be your father?"

Johnny looked smug. "My father wouldn't get sore if I played with Cathy. And what's he doing on TV? He's dead."

Dr. Cristo didn't pursue the point. He had heard enough for a starter. Enough to recommend that the new patient be led to the hydrotherapy ward. Wilkes, the attendant who had brought Johnny to Cristo's office for preliminary examination, took over.

Johnny was escorted into a large square room devoid of furniture save for two rows of covered bathtubs and tables of laboratory equipment. Other patients were being run through at the same time. Johnny pretended surprise at being one of the initiated. He smiled blankly as Wilkes watched two methodical attendants line up the canvas covers and adjust the machinery.

"Hydrotherapy, that's what you call this treatment I'm getting?"

"Yes," Wilkes said.

"Did Cathy come to visit me yet?"

"Your sister?"

Johnny nodded.

"Not yet," Wilkes said in a funny voice. "She'll probably come on visiting day."

"Confidentially, Mr. Wilkes, you really think this nerve-calming treatment will help me forget I want her in my arms?"

Wilkes' face was gentle.

"Undress, Mr. Barrett. This will really help relax you. See if I'm not right."

If Johnny had any doubts that he was a sane man, Wilkes' prognosis eradicated every last one of them. The fantastically icy water of the charged tub set his teeth on edge and his brain in mad revolt. He never did remember how much yelling and shouting he did until he was finally removed from the tub. Nor could he have given a coherent account of the bedlam that racketed like screaming hyenas all around him.

Later, much later it seemed, they let him go to the dining room. Sober, still cold, and feeling frozen, Johnny joined Pagliacci and the other patients at the table. Lloyd and Wilkes, looking like Good Humor salesmen, were moving among the tables, carrying two trays from which they were dispensing vitamins, pills and other strange items. Wilkes paused at their table and handed a sealed packet to Pagliacci.

"Take your anticunvulsant."

"Don't like it," Pagliacci said. "I'll have that one. The tranquilizing drug."

Wilkes sighed, set the tray down on the table and took the packet back from Pagliacci. Lloyd was busy at the next table. Wilkes split the packet with his fingernail and poured the contents into a paper cup of water. Pagliacci pretended not to notice and Johnny sensed something in the wind.

"I want a steak," Pagliacci continued, "the size of a cow. I hate my meat already cut up."

Wilkes handed him the cup. "Drink this."

Pagliacci sighed but took the cup. No sooner had he raised it to his lips when a patient at Lloyd's table jumped up, grabbed the cup from Pagliacci's hand, splattering him. He bellowed, "He took my vitamins!"

With a roar, Pagliacci raised himself, lifted the scrawny intruder by the elbows and flung him away, angrily. The man sailed into Lloyd, who in turn fell against the men seated around the table. It was a chain reaction of violence. An inmate shoved Lloyd hard. He cursed and blew his whistle. That did it. The dining room erupted with grating chairs, toppling tables and flying plates and cups. Someone started singing a wild loud tune. Patients milled about, swinging their arms and colliding. For a second, Johnny didn't know what to do. Then he spotted Stuart and it all came back.

Stuart was still sitting at his place, oblivious to the riot surrounding him, studying his map and several paper cups lined up like soldiers before him. Johnny struggled through the press of churning bodies and managed to reach Stuart's table.

"Stuart," Johnny said, "move your troops to the right and we'll flank McClellan's forces."

The man's head shot up. His eyes, lost in a young face, filled with suspicion, even antagonism. Johnny leaned over him. Stuart seemed about to protest when the fight reached the table. A body jarred the table and the cups went scattering. Johnny retrieved them and replaced them in front of Stuart. Another whistle shrilled.

"Then we hit Antietam," Johnny said. "And hit it hard."

Stuart restudied the cups. "You will address me as Sir!"

"A lieutenant general never sirs a general."

Stuart was still staring at the cups. "What lieutenant general?"

"Nathan Bedford Forrest."

The fight had slowed, the noise had abated somewhat as Stuart looked up slowly. Attendants were restoring order, calming the patients. Suddenly, Stuart was on his feet, standing smartly, saluting sharply. Johnny returned the salute.

"At ease, Jeb," Johnny commanded. "Report to my command post."

Lloyd was shouting now, his face livid. "On your feet! Everybody on your feet!" He blew the whistle hard.

Stuart was oblivious. His eyes shone. "Where

are you bivouacked, sir?" More shouting drowned out Johnny's reply.

"Where are you bivouacked, General Forrest?" Stuart repeated.

"A mile north of Gettysburg," Johnny snapped. "Ward B."

Wilkes' voice had joined Lloyd's in the fight to restore order. "March! Be quick now!"

For the first time, Stuart smiled. Then he about-faced, falling into the hasty line that was forming. Lloyd, Wilkes and the sweating attendants were making a hasty muster. Johnny fell in behind Stuart, scarcely hiding the jubilation soaring in his brain. The talk with Stuart had been a grade A success—he was making some real headway now.

The solution of the Sloan murder seemed closer than ever.

Dr. Cristo received Cathy in his office with mixed emotions. It was one thing to talk to the sister of a mentally deranged man but when that sister has a haunting face and figure plus the long, blonde hair of a goddess, it could be most disconcerting. Cristo was a man before he was anything else.

He watched her sit across from him, with her head held erect and her classic beauty in control, but he didn't like the haggard look of her eyes.

"We know about his fetish for your hair,"

Cristo said softly. "But did he ever try to cut it off?"

"Once."

"With a pair of scissors or a knife?"

"Scissors."

"Did he kiss you when he tried to cut off your hair?"

The doctor's monotone lulled her and she became confused.

"No! Uh—yes."

Cristo paused. "Did he ever attack any man who showed interest in you?"

"Yes."

"Do you love John?"

"Oh, yes!" Cathy, released from the lie only for one question, blurted the truth feelingly.

"More than just a brother?"

"What do you mean?" She reddened at that.

"Often these cases are developed through encouragement."

Cathy was too confused now to understand.

"What do you mean?"

"Forgive me for saying this, Miss Barrett, but there is something very strange about this case. You do not appear too cooperative."

Cathy tried to summon back her strength. The doctor sounded suspicious.

"I'm sorry, Dr. Cristo. When I got your message, I—I thought something happened to him. I—I wasn't prepared for this—"

"Inquisition?"

"No."

"But you thought of that word, didn't you?"

"Yes."

Cristo hid a frown. The girl was far too beautiful to be a simpleton about sex. Somewhere, sometime, someone must have tried.

"Was John jealous of the way you revealed your body to other men?"

"Yes," she said blankly.

"Thank you for your time, Miss Barrett. That will be quite enough for now."

Cathy's relief flooded her face. "Can I see him now?"

"You'll have to wait for visiting day. Sorry."

Cathy bit her red lips. "How is he coming along?"

Dr. Cristo pyramided his fingers. "He's been uncommunicative all week, living inside his own private world. He's in dance therapy now. I believe that will help him out of his silent isolation."

"Dance therapy?"

"Yes. We were pleased when he even asked to attend the class."

Cathy, baffled, picked her white gloves off her lap, and stood up to say goodbye to Dr. Cristo.

The dance therapy class had struck Johnny Barrett as a great idea.

Besides keeping some of the hours occupied, there was a chance for wonderful human interest in the situation. He had discovered that volunteer teachers, who were also professional dancers, donated their free time to teaching the mentally ill that their stored-up feelings could be expressed in movement. Not that Johnny would have been interested in a madman doing the twist, say, but the possibilities were tremendous.

There just had to be a story in it. If the waltz, fox trot or samba could make a lunatic feel better, that was worth some copy.

The young woman instructing the class was a looker. A slim, disciplined brunette with long hair like Cathy's. Johnny was the first inmate to step forward when she asked for a dancing partner to assist in her demonstration.

Six male and six female patients were attending the class. And Stuart, oddly enough. But the farm boy was only an observer, standing with his back to the far wall, his eyes stony and cold.

Johnny was surprised at the female patients. They seemed so unfeminine and unpretty. As though being mentally deficient had somehow robbed them of their gender.

"One and two and three and four," the teacher called rhythmically, fairly leading Johnny around on the floor. The inmates gawked.

A piano was playing in the corner, fingered by the young teacher's associate, a middle-aged balding man who said nothing. Johnny kept his eyes on Stuart as he danced. Stuart, standing silently. Stuart, hearing the faraway drums of the Civil War.

"One and two and three and four," the teacher parroted as Johnny swept her around the studio in a waltz. The other couples followed, miming their movements, watching the teacher and Johnny like hawks, never taking their eyes away even as their bodies traveled. Johnny kept his vigil on Stuart. The tinny piano tinkled mercilessly.

The teacher smiled up at Johnny. She hadn't missed his focus on Stuart.

"Who's the man over there?"

"Stuart. He never communicates with anybody."

"Does he want to dance?" The teacher was so eager to help. Fresh, young and unworried. Johnny had a fast notion.

"I've got an idea how to get him to dance."

"I'm game. Anything you say."

"Follow me, Teacher."

He waltzed her to the piano, trying to forget how much he wished he had his arms around Cathy. But it was no good thinking of Cathy in the daytime. No good thinking about that fantastic womanly body at all. There was still Stuart and the story.

At the piano, Johnny whispered his plan. The teacher smiled and imparted it to the piano player. He grunted in acknowledgment, nodding as they swirled by. Subtly, without a change of tempo, the piano went into *Dixie*. Johnny watched for the effect on Stuart.

He had turned from the wall to face the music. His eyes came alive. "One and two and three and four . . ." caroled the instructress. Stuart began to keep time with his feet, his fingers tapping his thighs. Johnny drew closer to him, bringing the young teacher abreast of their target. She smiled at Stuart and held out her arms to him.

Almost on cue, Stuart stepped forward, encircled her waist in his arm and carried her away from Johnny. The lilting strains of *Dixie* in waltz tempo filled the room. Stuart twirled proudly about the room.

When the piano ceased, the dance was done.

Stuart joined Johnny, his face beaming.

"I'm thirsty," he said.

"I'll get some water," Johnny said, sensing that Stuart was becoming used to him. That was good. A trusting man was better than a suspicious one when you needed information.

The water cooler was empty. Johnny fumed, then decided to go into the next ward to get some. It wouldn't do to disappoint Stuart now.

Once he stepped out of the dance therapy class and went ten paces, turning into the next ward door, he walked into another world.

A frightening, terrifying universe into which no man should ever step.

There were women staring at him. Gaunt women, fleshy women, women with eyes that devoured him. Johnny gaped and tried to back away. The room throbbed with something animal and alien.

There was very nearly a smell of the jungle.

It took Johnny three seconds to realize he had stumbled into the nympho ward.

He tried to back out the door. Locked. It had slammed shut. Behind him, a growl sounded. More animal than human. He whirled, bringing his hands up for protection. The beady-eyed women, he was too frightened to count them, were circling him warily. Their red tongues licked, their naked eyes gleamed. One of them, an enormous blonde, bared her breasts with both hands and began to croon to him, her eyes never leaving his face.

Suddenly, the most gaunt of the women jumped forward and planted a moist kiss on his cheek. A bosomy redhead shoved her out of the way and flung her arms about Johnny's neck. Dazed, he tried to pound on the locked door. They closed in on him.

The damp press of their bodies against him was delirium. Breasts crushed his face. Wet mouths suckled at his shoulders, tore at his uniform. He felt teeth sink into his exposed neck. He screamed and hit out. Somebody cursed. Another laughed. A gorgeous nympho with straggly hair.

"He's mine! I saw him first!"

"No! No! Mine! Mine!"

Johnny gathered his throat muscles, screaming.

The women panted, tugged and tore, bearing him to the floor of the ward. They cast aside their own flimsy garments and smothered him in their naked ugliness. Johnny's brain exploded as he gasped for air.

A gorgeous face loomed before him. Wild eyes beseeched him. "You're mine, mine, mine, all mine—"

A woman shouted like a rooster. The room spun in a crazy carousel of shrieks, pants and moans of desire. The tide of surging women engulfed Johnny Barrett.

He clawed for air under the pile of writhing bodies. His nostrils were charged with the stench of terror, his stomach seething with the sickness of decay.

The gorgeous nympho pressed her body to his face, butting him with her exposed breasts. He twisted his face. A madwoman raked him with her nails, her eyes popping sadistically.

The world reeled dizzily, urged on by the hoarse shouts of the women of the nympho ward.

The wind blew dust along the ground into his mouth as he sang.
Paul Bowles, **The Delicate Prey**

THE CELL

JOHNNY BARRETT was sitting in "The Street" when Stuart found him. Stuart was happy. *Dixie* trilled from his mouth in a piping whistle. Johnny, plastered with bandages about the neck and face, looked up at him wanly. Pagliacci was idly standing nearby explaining an aria from *La Boheme* to a patient Johnny didn't know. Johnny had found "The Street" peaceful today, after the madness of yesterday.

Stuart smiled down at him.

"I heard about you getting wounded at Shiloh. Hurt much? I'll get the mess sergeant to fix you up some baked apple."

"Thanks. I'm okay. My cavalry, led by Colonels Wilkes and Lloyd, saved me."

Stuart was far away again. He leaned forward, elbows on his knees, his head cupped in his hands.

"Last time I had baked apple was in Japan."

Johnny's ears pricked up. *Japan.* That meant Korea.

"How far is that from Shiloh, Jeb?"

"Japan ain't in this country. It's far away. In Asia." Stuart peeked out from the cup of his hands. "Is that Buddha still there?"

"What Buddha?" Johnny asked quietly, forgetting his cuts and bruises.

"I keep seeing the great Buddha of Kamakura," Stuart said tonelessly. "And he keeps looking at me. I want to climb up a parallel to his head. So's I can look down on the people praying for my battalion."

It was obvious now that Stuart was trapped in his own mental hell. Johnny watched him closely, prodded him gently as he knew a psychiatrist might.

"Big Buddha, Jeb?"

Stuart nodded. "I keep seeing monks in a parade. And all the little girls dressed like baby geishas going to prayer to ask Buddha to take care of me when I go back to Korea."

"Korea?"

"I got a week's leave. Spent it in Japan." His face came up from his hands and he grasped the front of Johnny's shirt. "How did I get up on that playground?"

"Don't you know?" Johnny didn't move a muscle, hoping that the patients on "The Street" would remain orderly and not cause a rumpus that would bring the guards and halt Stuart's narrative.

"It's on the roof of the world and the wheels keep turning around and around. Just like the

Commies kept running round and round us on that hill in Korea."

Johnny held his breath. Korea was the beginning of all of Stuart's mental history.

"There's all kinds of games in Japan. Toy games... toy trains... train!... Mount Fuji ... No! Another train! Another train! Another train!" He had collapsed again, breathing hard into his cupped hands.

Stuart raised his head. His eyes were now sane.

"We were supposed to sandbag a train in Korea... but we were captured. It was cold and they marched us in the snow—" His eyes saw Johnny for the first time, really. "Who are *you*?"

"Johnny Barrett."

"You in my outfit?"

"No."

"What is this place?"

"A mental hospital."

"Tokyo?"

"The States. War's been over for years."

Stuart looked surprised. "This an army nut house?"

"No."

"How'd I get in *here*?"

"Don't you remember?"

Stuart shook his head.

"You became a Commie in Korea," Johnny said flatly.

There was a short silence in which Stuart tried to think.

"You're one of the nuts here, aren't you?"

"Yes," Johnny said.

"Figures. You've got to be crazy to call me a Commie."

"It's on the record, Stuart. You enlisted June 6, 1951 and were captured November 18, 1951."

Stuart's pale face showed a slight flush.

"You're making it up about me turning Red!"

"Returned prisoners of war said you informed on fellow prisoners."

"That's a lie!" Stuart shouted.

"You became a member of the 'Kremlin Club,'" Johnny said, pouring it on deliberately now.

Stuart seized his shirt front again. "Don't you call me a Commie!"

"In 1954 you were still behind the Iron Curtain."

"I told you to stop that talk." Stuart half-rose.

"You told your father the Reds were your friends."

Stuart sat down again. "I wrote *Pappy?*"

"You wrote him that Korea was an American imperialist war planned by Wall Street."

Stuart laughed. "You *must* be off your rocker, boy. Why should I write my Pappy when he can't read? He's a tenant farmer. He can't read or write. He—" Chagrin swept over his face. "Wonder if he's still alive—"

"He's alive," Johnny said.

"How do you know?" Stuart demanded belligerently.

"He's still got that redbone hound of yours."

Stuart's eyes warmed up wistfully at mention of the dog.

"I remember helping Pappy sharecrop on another man's land when I ran away and joined the Army. You're right. That was 1951. June 6. Seventh anniversary of D-Day in Normandy. I remember like it was today. But why did I run away from home? I liked my home. That's a downright lie." He matched stares with Johnny, his face working. Then his voice picked up again.

"I know why I went over to the side of the Commies. From the time I was a kid, my folks fed me bigotry for breakfast and ignorance for supper. Illiterate religious fanatics spouting bitterness and hate. I could've gone to school but Pappy made it easy for me not to go. He never went. Why should I?" His eyes misted. "Never—not once—did they make me feel proud of where I was born. That's the cancer they put into me. No knowledge of my country. No pride. Just a hymn of hate. *Njong yee* the Chinese Reds call it. *Nenavidet* the Russians call it."

Johnny Barrett's reportorial brain was in seventh heaven.

"The Commies," Stuart murmured, "drummed it into me that ignorance was the root of every evil. And when I thought of Pappy, they were right. He loved nobody. Not Ma or me or himself. I'd have defected to *any* enemy and the Commies made it easy because my brain was cabbage and they learned me all about life from cabbages to commisars and gave me a woman and she called me mister and made me feel important and it was easy to go over to their side because they said I wouldn't grow up ignorant like Pappy."

He paused, caught up in the past. Johnny waited.

"They gave me pretty good clothes to wear and everybody called me smart when I made a speech on television the day I left the interior for China. That was the day I refused repatriation and I got a lot of rewards. Whiskey, marijuana . . . y'know I was captured the first day in combat. November 18, 1951."

Johnny coughed. "What changed your mind about the Reds?"

"A dogface." Memory made Stuart smile. "I was having a ball waving the Red flag until the day I met a retread from World War Two. A sergeant out of the First Division, fought in North Africa, Sicily, all through Europe to Czechoslovakia. When he was captured in Korea, he was sent to my camp and I was assigned to brainwash him to the Commie side." Stuart's smile faded. "This sergeant—Sergeant Kolowicz was his name—he told me things I never knew. Things that sent shivers down my back. Things to wrap up gentle and proud like and go to sleep still thinking about. Things that gave me a feeling . . . things my folks should've learned me. And then I wanted to go home."

Johnny waited. The break in the wall was coming.

"I stopped waving the Red flag and they thought I was sick in the head and it was easy to get back here on the next prisoner exchange and I was dishonorably discharged and nobody wanted to talk to me. People spit at me and Pappy spit at me and the newspapers kept hounding me and hounding me—" Stuart covered his face again. Now was the time, Johnny thought.

"Stuart, I've got to ask you something."

"Think they'll let me out of this place now that I'm all right?" The hopeful face poised before him broke his heart but there was no stopping now.

"Did you see the man who killed Sloan in the kitchen?"

Stuart stared at Johnny. "Sure I did."

"Who was it?"

"I was under the table with two men," Stuart recited strangely. "What was I doing under the table? I couldn't see his face but I saw he was wearing white pants." Stuart's eyes filmed over, the old glassy look returning. "White pants! White fence! Stone wall!"

This time his fierce shouts disturbed the men in "The Street." They turned startled faces toward Stuart. Pagliacci rumbled in his throat. Stuart had leaped to the top of a bench, his face contorted. Johnny was helpless to stop him.

"Lee! We got to help General Lee!" Stuart was yelling. "Come on, let's get them damn Yankees!"

The rebel yell that broke from his corded throat reverberated off the walls of the corridor. The men in "The Street" simply stared.

Johnny Barrett could only think of one thing. *White pants.*

The murderer of Sloan had been wearing white pants.

He told Cathy all about it when she came to see him on the very first visiting day. Cathy, pale but vibrantly beautiful, peered closely at him through the mesh wire screen that separated them. Johnny's eyes were curiously excited and gleaming. Cathy controlled her nerves, remembering the printed sign posted over the entrance: *Visitors Will Refrain from Exciting Patients.* It was hysterical, that sign. All around the room, Cathy could hear chuckling, sobbing and wails of grief. It was a tough road to hoe. Seeing a loony relative, lover or husband. Watching Johnny was putting her through the wringer as it was. She wanted to kiss him, hug him, squeeze him, ask him how he really felt. But Johnny, once the sturdiest Romeo of them all could only talk about his damn story.

"The killer is an attendant or a doctor," he whispered. "Stuart couldn't see his face but he saw white pants. Tell Swanee one of the two other witnesses will open up too. I feel it."

Another weird laugh sounded on their left. Wilkes and Lloyd, standing on quiet guard behind them, were silent and noncommittal. Cathy restrained a shudder. She felt her nerves slipping away like noisy mice, rustling all the way. The room was loaded with tragedy.

Next to her was a patient who couldn't stop

laughing. His mother, grey-haired and worn, was sobbing into a handkerchief. Across from them, a patient was whispering into his son's ear. The young boy seemed to be a son anyway. What other male relative would come to see a mental case? Cathy turned back to Johnny, pressing her face against the mesh toward his mouth. He pulled back, baffling her. Then he smiled and gingerly patted his bruised mouth.

"Lips still hurt, honey. Those females almost bit them off."

Cathy wanted to ask about that too but Wilkes was intoning the words of authority: "Visiting time over. That's all, folks."

There was a scrape of chairs. Visitors began to file past. The weird laughter erupted again, backgrounded by sobbing. Cathy stood up, all of her body cold and foreign. Her eyes found Johnny's. He looked like a conspiratorial kid again.

"The killer is an attendant or a doctor," he whispered. "Stuart couldn't see his face but he saw the white pants. Tell Swanee one of the other two witnesses will open up too. I feel it."

It was only when she realized that he had repeated word for word what he had said once before that the full horror of the situation came home to her. Stunned, she could only wave goodbye in a vague gesture.

Johnny waved back and Cathy stumbled past Wilkes out into the hall for a breath of fresh air.

The horror was growing and it was taking her Johnny with it.

Swanee didn't believe her when she poured

out her terrible suspicion in the office of the *Globe*. Even with the chattering of typewriters and the ringing of phones, Cathy still felt the awful chill of the mental hospital.

Swanee scoffed loudly from his desk. "If he went down into a coal mine on a disaster story he'd come up with a little coal dirt on his face, wouldn't he?"

"He's getting sick."

"He's doing great. Been there only six weeks and narrowed the hunt down to an employee, didn't he? Something the cops couldn't do." The pride in Swanee's voice sickened Cathy.

"If you don't phone Dr. Cristo right this minute and get Johnny out of that place tonight, I will."

Swanee tilted back in his chair, too secure in the power of the press to mind her fears.

"You're becoming a nervous wreck, Cathy. I'm more worried about you outside than Johnny inside."

"Call Cristo!" Cathy screamed, coming apart.

Swanee grunted and moved the phone toward her with emphasis.

"You call him. Call Dr. Cristo and you'll lose Johnny for good. And you *know* it."

Cathy stared down at the telephone, powerless to touch it. Swanee was right. Damn him, he was always right.

Johnny's headaches began to get more frequent following Cathy's first visit. They came on him at night, attacking what little reserve was left over from the supply necessary for his waking masquerade as a mental patient. Ward B became a hell-hole of raging headache and sweaty nights of aching agony. Nothing seemed to help. Neither aspirin or even Pagliacci's prescription of chewing gum. Johnny Barrett got very little sleep. His reflexes became ragged, his nerves awry. Some days he was hard put to remember his mission; the physical demands of his body robbing his brain of all sorts of deductive activity.

Wilkes talked to him in the corridor one day about it. Word had gotten around about Johnny's violent headaches. A trip to the psychiatrist was the first remedy anybody could think of.

"How long've I been here, Wilkes?"

"Nine weeks."

Time sure flew. Johnny shook his head. There was something he couldn't remember.

"You're not going to put me into the Hole, are you?"

"Nah. Only one patient in there now. Colored man. He thinks he's white." They were passing the door of the Hole. Johnny stared at the small opening in the door.

"What did he do?"

"Beat up a Negro in Ward D."

Johnny's mind flicked. *Trent. It must be Trent. No wonder I haven't seen him around. But where is the other witness—Boden? I've got to be careful about asking about either of them.*

"More tests for me, Wilkes?"

"Just something to help you with your headaches." They had come to another door in the long corridor. John halted. *I don't remember telling them about my headaches.*

Wilkes held the door open, smiling.

"Nothing in there to hurt you. Go on in."

Johnny hesitated. "Last time I went into a strange room I was attacked by Amazons."

Wilkes grinned. "That's a secret dream most men have."

"Yeah? You try it sometime and tell me about it."

Once in the room, Johnny Barrett remembered no more. His head started splitting and he tumbled into a merciful oblivion, broken only by wave upon wave of relaxing sensations of rising and falling.

He opened his eyes to find Dr. Cristo standing before him.

They had strapped him to a hard table which tilted his body backward at a forty-five degree angle. He was naked save for a towel compress around his lower half. The table seemed to be equipped with all kinds of tubes and wiring and dials. Cristo was pressing a button, checking figures and colored lights on a calculation board.

"Something wrong?" Johnny heard himself say. He felt fine. Not even alarmed.

"No," Cristo said, studying the instruments. "Just saw a twitch of one of your muscles."

"The one in my head?"

"Tell me, John. Is your desire for your sister still as strong as ever?"

"Take me off this ironing board and I'll share my dreams with you. I'm cold and sweating."

"Chill sweats are usual in your case," Dr. Cristo explained blandly.

"What's my case?" The lights on the board were dancing again.

"You understand the word puberty?"

Careful. Smells like a trap. "You tell me."

Cristo spaced his answer. "Sexual maturity."

"I knew it all along," Johnny laughed.

Cristo pursed his lips. "You're suffering from a form of dementia praecox incident to the age of puberty, characterized by childish behavior, hallucinations and emotional deterioration."

Which makes me a hebephrenic schizophrenic. Or Doc Fong is no expert.

"Just for the record, Doc. What am I?"

"A hebephrenic schizophrenic, John."

"Is that bad?"

"It's not good, John."

Dr. Cristo could not see Johnny Barrett smile inwardly. So far, so good. He was still his own man and the headaches would go away. A guy was bound to get headaches in a nut factory, spending nine weeks with abnormal loonies. It wasn't exactly Fun House.

Johnny, boy, Johnny Barrett told himself, *they were just ordinary headaches after all. You're still ahead of the game.*

"Unstrap him, Wilkes," Dr. Cristo said. "You can go back to the ward now, John."

The lights on the panel board had stopped blinking.

Does not everything depend on our interpretation of the silence around us?
*Lawrence Durrel, **Justine***

THE HOLE

CATHY in leotards would have driven any man to wild dreams of conquest. For a man in Johnny Barrett's state of mind, she would have been unbearable. Therefore, it was good that only Swanee saw her the morning she was rehearsing on the small stage at the club.

Music was supplied by a record player. Cathy had enveloped her statuesque figure in dark leotards which clung to her curves like mucilage. Her long, luxuriant hair was a tumbling pile of gold. Swanee watched her admiringly when he came in.

Cathy saw him, and broke her dance, her face wrinkling.

"Did you make Johnny change his mind?"

Swanee's wag was negative. "I tried. But he's too close to the story now. That ex-GI, Stuart, has been transferred to another floor. But Johnny's certain Trent or Boden will open up."

She reached for a towel, forlornly.

"Was Dr. Fong with you?"

"Uh huh."

"What did *he* say?" Cathy mopped her face. A fine sheen of dampness made her skin glow.

"That it's only natural for Johnny to show mental strain."

"What else?"

"That's it."

Cathy's eyes narrowed. "Want me to check with Dr. Fong myself?"

Swanee growled helplessly. "Well . . . he's afraid that the force driving Johnny can boomerang."

"Meaning he could snap, is that it?" Swanee would never know the pang those words cost her.

Swanee raised his hands. "Don't jump to conclusions. If I pulled him off now he'd still suffer from some kind of depressive psychosis because he'd never know what would have happened if he had stuck it out long enough to contact the other two witnesses."

Cathy stood stock-still, her heart jumping.

"You mean if he quits—that depression sickness could hit him?"

"Yes."

"But if he cracks the murder he'll be all right, won't he?"

"Yes."

She threw back her head in scorn. "Do you seriously believe that?"

"Yes."

"You're crazy!"

Swanee stared at her for a long, poignant moment. He turned without further comment and stalked through the tables toward the exit.

Cathy went over to the record player and picked the playing arm off the record. She had hardly heard the music. Her head was full of Swanee's words, her heart full of ache for Johnny. Her limbs felt dead. What a waste. It was all such a waste.

The tears trickled down her lovely face.

Johnny Barrett sat in the long corridor called "The Street" at "make-friends time" and watched and waited. Dr. Fong was so right. He had said it all about insanity. You only had to look around you at the poor old faces of the inmates. Lost souls committed years before their time; committed before the state put teeth into the law. Men railroaded by relatives to save a buck and get them out of the way. Johnny could hear the refrain: *"Grandpa will love it there. It's like a home. Three meals a day and so many people his own age to talk to."*

He watched the bony man draw closer to him. The guy's eyes were two burning lumps of coal. He looked down at Johnny, his hands closed over his stomach.

"Don't you dare strike me," he protested in a womanish voice. "I'm pregnant. I've been carrying my baby for five months."

Johnny did not smile and the bony patient moved on.

The Street was alive with curiosity today. The walkers, the leaners, the sitters, the squatters, the talkers were all lined up on each side of the corridor. It was like a scene from some picture of hell as envisioned by some modern artist.

Johnny saw the sign before he saw the handsome young Negro patient who was holding it and marching forward proudly. INTEGRATION AND DEMOCRACY DON'T MIX. GO HOME, NIGGER. With a start, Johnny recognized the defiant toss of that head, the flaming intensity of the face. Witness Number Two to the murder of Sloan was out of The Hole. Trent.

Trent. Only Negro student in a Southern university. His mind broken by the ordeal. Believes he's white, hates Negroes, thinks he's the head of the White Citizen's Council and head of the KKK.

Before he could reach Johnny's bench, Lloyd and Wilkes had hurried forward, checking patients and then stopping at either side of Trent who had been proceeding in an orderly fashion.

"Trent," Lloyd snapped peevishly.

"Yes, sir?" Johnny heard the scorn in Trent's reply.

"A pillow case is missing."

"I don't have it, sir."

"It's from your bed."

"I don't have it, sir."

Lloyd's hand tightened on the elbow holding the placard aloft. "You want to go back into The Hole?"

"I don't have it, sir." It was like some well-rehearsed litany.

Wilkes made a gesture at Lloyd. "Let him keep it."

"Keep out of this, Wilkes," Lloyd barked.

"Dr. Cristo said not to get him excited." Wilkes' kindly face was concerned. Trent stood his ground, staring mutely ahead, holding high the placard.

Lloyd snarled, "You know what that pillow case means."

Wilkes ignored him and smiled at Trent. "It's all right, Trent. We know you don't have it."

"Thank you, sir."

The Negro walked on with his placard. Lloyd glared at his back, then said something to Wilkes that Johnny couldn't catch. Trent marched past. Johnny rose to his feet carefully and followed. The attendants had gone back the way they had come.

Trent did not walk far. He found another bench and sat down, facing the sign front and center. There was another patient on the bench but he was remote from everything. Johnny managed to sit down next to Trent without crowding him. Trent was staring straight ahead now but the other patient was frozen into immobility, his left hand held out like the fixed branch of a great tree.

On the floor near the bench, another patient lay curled like a grotesque question mark, arms clasped over his eyes.

Johnny stared at the man holding out his arm. Trent saw the look.

"He does that everv day," he said in a liquidly powerful voice. "He's reaching out for his nerves."

"Friend of yours?" Johnny asked softly.

"No," Trent answered just as softly. "He's a nigger lover. He didn't make his kid spit on a black boy. God punished him. That's why he's in such a catatonic stupor. Watch this."

Trent reached out with his placard and used it to tilt the catatonic's outstretched hand above his head. When he lowered the placard, the catatonic's arm was still high above his head, as rigid as that same tree branch.

"Now he's the Statue of Liberty." Trent's eyes fastened on Johnny. "What are you doing here?"

"Visiting a friend."

"So am I, friend. So am I. Let's take a walk down The Street."

Johnny could see that Trent used the walking time to display his placard of protest. They filed slowly past the defeats lined up on either side of the corridor.

"The Hole's for dangerous and troublesome people," Trent offered from nowhere. "They put me in by mistake."

"So I heard."

"No, you didn't. I just told you."

"That's right."

Trent's chuckle was melodious. "I know why you're shining up to me. You want to carry my sign."

"No, I don't."

"You calling me a liar?"

"No."

"Go make your own sign and carry it. You coming to the meeting?"

"What meeting?"

Trent had paused at that, to think hard.

"I forgot," Trent admitted. "Do you know the conductor of the State Symphony Orchestra?"

"No." Johnny was finding it difficult to keep up with the man's quicksilver mind.

"I do. He comes here now and then as guest conductor of our own hospital band. I like him but he's mixed up. He permits a black boy to play with white musicians." Trent shrugged. "Oh, they're all right as *entertainers.*"

They walked on. Johnny's mind was seething with the paradox of this solid Negro mouthing the dictum of the bigoted white.

But suddenly Trent had halted again, his eyes popping, leveling a long arm down the hall. "Let's get that nigger before he marries my daughter!"

Johnny couldn't move in time. Trent had hurled himself at an old, withered Negro patient, striking with his placard. The old man recoiled. Only the fact that Johnny could pull Trent back enabled him to escape through a door nearby. Wilkes and Lloyd reappeared magically again. Trent looked down at the floor.

"What's the trouble now?" Lloyd bellowed sarcastically.

Johnny answered. "No trouble, Mr. Lloyd."

"What are you hatching now, Trent?"

"He didn't—"

Lloyd poked Johnny with a finger. "I'm talking to *him.*"

Wilkes sighed. "Are you feeling all right, Trent?"

"Yes, sir," Trent said in the voice he had used before.

"No trouble now, Trent," Wilkes pleaded. "Promise?"

"Yes, sir."

Trent looked at Johnny when the attendants moved on.

"Thank you, friend."

"It's all right, friend."

They jockeyed past several patients and found a spot where they could be alone. Trent peered furtively about, propped his placard against the wall and squatted on the floor. Johnny sat beside him. Trent checked the corridor once again, then tugged a pillow case out from under his shirt. Johnny recognized it almost immediately. There were holes gouged in the cloth. Holes for the eyes, nose and mouth.

Trent was busy with a pencil, etching a circle and a crude cross above the two holes that were cut out parallel for the eyes.

"What are you doing?" Johnny asked, not needing an answer.

"The sign of the Invisible Empire," Trent clucked solemnly. "That's a cyclos. From the Greek word Kuklos. Means circle." With that, he slipped the hood over his head, staring at Johnny through the eyeholes.

"This baptizes a new organization—the Ku Klux."

"Sounds good," Johnny said.

"No! Ku Klux *Klan!* More mysterious, more menacing, more alliterative. Ku Klux Klan. Say it."

"Ku Klux Klan."

"KKK," Trent said rapidly.

"KKK," Johnny repeated, just as quickly.

Trent glowed. "It'll catch on quick. We'll drive those carpetbaggers back North. Scare the hell out of them. Tar and feather them. Hang them. Burn them. Who are you?"

"Your friend?"

Trent's hooded head was menacing. "I don't know you."

Johnny's mind raced. Stuart. The South. It would work again. " 'I got here fustest,' " he beban to quote.

Trent finished the famous quotation with him, jubilantly. " '—with the mostest!' " Trent's voice rose happily. "General Forrest! Nathan Bedford Forrest!"

He saluted sharply. Johnny saluted back. Suddenly, Trent's handsome dark face was visible again and he angrily tugged the hood off. His face was inches from Johnny's.

"General, you're going around taking credit for founding the KKK. *I'm* the founder. *I'm* the Grand Wizard. What's our code word?"

"Secrecy."

"General, if Christ walked the streets of my home town he'd be horrified. You've never seen so many niggers cluttering up the cafes and schools and buses and washrooms. I'm for pure Americanism. White supremacy!"

As his voice rose in crescendo, Trent hopped to the bench, his arms pistoning up and down. Johnny watched. The patients, lethargic, lost in their private hells, gazed up mutely at the hoarsely exhorting Trent.

"Listen to me, Americans! America for

Americans! We've got to throw rocks and hurl bombs—black bombs for the black foreigners. So they like hot music, do they? We'll give them a crescendo they'll never forget. Burn that Freedom Bus. Burn those Fredom Riders. Burn any man who serves them at a lunch counter. Burn every dirty nigger-loving pocketbook integrationist!"

The still, silent men circled in closer. Johnny was caught with them, held by the sweeping fury of this mad orator.

"Collect a lot of blackjacks and good lengths of pipe and we'll show those African rabble-rousers they can't breathe our white air and go to school with our white children. Get some inflammable liquid and pour it on them and their homes and their pickaninnies and set them on fire. Call the members of the White Citizens Council. Call the KKK. We'll sponsor the niggers North, get rid of every black mother's son and daughter. America for Americans!"

One of the patients utttered a slow, Southern drawl. "America for Americans!"

Trent pinned him with a dedicated glare. "Keep our schools white!"

"That's right," the Southerner yelled. "Keep 'em white!"

"I'm against Catholics!" roared Trent.

"Hallelujah, man!"

"Against Jews!"

"Hallelujah!"

The patients began to rumble, murmur and come awake like some sleeping ocean that has been suddenly disturbed by a gathering wind.

"Against niggers!" Trent's voice cannonaded. Johnny stood transfixed.

"Hallelujah!" the Southern patient echoed.

Suddenly, Trent leveled an arm. "There's one!" He slipped the pillow case quickly over his head. "Let's get that black boy before he marries my daughter!"

The Southerner flung back his head and a terrifying, ear-splitting Rebel yell filled the corridor. The patients galvanized. Trent, screaming "Hallelujah!" plunged down the hall. The patients clamored behind him, excited to fever pitch by the drugging power of Trent's mighty voice. Johnny was swept like a whirlwind with the headlong charge.

The hapless ancient Negro patient, spotted once more by Trent, turned and ran from the mob rushing toward him with meaningless looks of anger, exaltation and defiance on their multiple faces. Johnny ran, too. Trying to catch up with Trent, to stop him, to keep him from getting thrown into The Hole again. Trent might be the key to the murder of Sloan—

Whistles shrilled. Patients screamed. The Rebel yell thundered off the walls of the corridor. In a maze of twisting grey bodies and grey faces, Johnny saw Wilkes, Lloyd and a Negro attendant flying forward like a team of football players to meet Trent's charge.

Johnny reached Trent just in time.

The Negro attendant was poised to strike him with a club of some kind. Johnny batted the hand away. Trent shrieked another phrase of racial hatred. Wilkes and Lloyd grabbed him and Johnny grabbed them. Suddenly, Lloyd had pinned Johnny's arms in a vise and the whole picture changed. Johnny fought back. Lloyd's hands on him were like some violation of individual rights and glories. Johnny lashed out. He squirmed, kicked and twisted. He never heard the violent words that flamed from his own throat. He only saw Trent's black, steaming face, bobbing like a jack-o'-lantern in the crush of bodies.

He never saw the punch that rocketed him down the long corridor into darkness.

Darkness, unremitting.

The ceiling never changed.

Night or day, it made no difference. The ceiling remained a meaningless square of drab gloom. The Hole had lived up to advance notice. The first time Johnny Barrett opened his eyes and was unable to move, he didn't panic. He pieced it all out very carefully. They had placed him on a bed of sorts, bound him in a straitjacket and left him to study the ceiling and think about things. The only thing worth cheering about was that they hadn't separated him from Trent.

Trent lay alongside of him, on a similar bed, similarly bound. Johnny had only to twist his head around to recognize Trent's dark, chiseled profile.

The Hole was quiet. You felt muffled in cotton or like a moth ball tucked away in a clothes closet. No outside sounds registered on the hearing. The hours were maddeningly slow.

Three nights now. Still not a word out of Trent. I thought it was a break being cooped up with him alone. I'm getting nowhere fast. When

I get back to the ward, I'll concentrate on Boden. He's got to open up. A scientist with an I.Q. of 170 should have a couple of sane moments for me . . .

"Wednesday, August 30, 1954," Trent said suddenly in the gloom. Johnny tensed, senses immediately alerted. It was the first time Trent had spoken in these three days.

"Go on, Trent," Johnny said aloud. "Keep talking."

"Wednesday, August 30, 1954. Wednesday. W-e-d-n-e-s—"

"Go on, Trent."

The deep voice lifted.

"Wednesday, August 30, 1954, the U.S. Supreme Court decreed that the nation's schools must be racially desegregated with all deliberate speed. I'm a boy in the Amazon jungle—"

Johnny cursed softly. The damn twists and turns of the lunatic mind were baffling.

"—a brown boy, not a black boy, and someone is scraping my thigh with the teeth of the piranha fish to change my blood to white blood. Wednesday, August 30, 1954, the U.S. Supreme Court decreed a ceremonial dance to be racially desegregated with all deliberate speed—here comes the KKK! Run! Run! Run for your life, Trent! I can't see his face, I can't see his face. Run, run, run—"

The hoarse shout of Trent's voice made Johnny close his eyes in defeat. What was the use? Lunatics never—

He was unprepared for the sight of Trent sitting bolt upright in bed, staring around with real bewilderment on his face, looking puzzled. Johnny's optimism returned.

"Always in color," Trent said in a normal voice. "The same nightmare always in color. Strange how I always get my mind back after that dream—" He peered at Johnny, his bound arms bracing. "Wonder what he's in for?"

Johnny opened his eyes. "We got into a race riot. You leading, me trying to save your neck."

Trent gaped. "You don't sound sick to me."

"Neither do you."

Trent shook his head. "Sometimes I'm even lucid for five minutes after that nightmare."

"Like right now?"

"Like right now. Do *you* come back after a nightmare?"

"Yes."

"Is it in color?"

Johnny controlled his elation. "Yes."

"Something distorted?"

"Yes."

"What's your name?"

"Johnny Barrett."

"Barrett." Trent tasted the word. "That's a good name. Elizabeth Barrett . . . I like her *Chaucer Modernized* . . . I wanted to be like her. Or Browning. A poet . . . a writer . . . a scholar."

Johnny fed the rationality. "She was only twelve when she wrote *The Battle of Marathon.*"

"Eleven," Trent corrected. They both laughed. The sound was good in the drabness of The Hole.

"Eleven, twelve," Trent said. "What's the difference? Nobody stopped her from studying

Greek or Latin or putting her dreams onto paper. She never had to wear her face on her sleeve like I had to wear my race on mine. So you know I was the guinea pig in the classroom, eh?"

"The whole country went to school with you every day, Trent."

"I failed," he said miserably. "Couldn't take the pressure. Know the long corridor in this hospital? The one we call The Street? There was a corridor like that in the school. It was rough walking past the students in that corridor, Johnny."

"A lot of people were counting on you."

"A lot of people didn't have to walk that corridor every day. How long have I been in The Hole?"

"Three days." Johnny bit his lip. They were getting so close to the moment of truth.

"Did I kill anyone in the race riot?"

"No."

"Hurt anyone?" Trent sounded dismayed.

"Almost. Wilkes and Lloyd got these streamlined coats on us before any bones could be broken."

"Sorry I got you involved."

"Forget that. Why didn't you go to France for an education?"

"Oh, I could have left the country and become an expatriate in Paris with a beard and an accent but—would *you* have gone to Paris?"

"I never had to walk through a segregated white school with classmates spitting at me."

Trent craned his head toward Johnny.

"No, the Left Bank's crowded with Negro

exiles and I didn't want racial discrimination to give me the initial push toward self-exile because my roots are here. I feel that one day the whites will forget the color of my skin as they forgot they burned white women in Salem.... I tried to get used to it. But I just couldn't. And just going to school to get an education broke the ice. I had ulcers and eggs and ulcers and geography and ulcers and potatoes and ulcers and history and ulcers and pie. I know it's an accident of birth and yet those ulcers kept increasing. I could have been born yellow or white but luck picked me black and I'm not proud and I'm ashamed."

"What are you now, Trent?"

"Just angry. Angry enough to want to go to school in my own country, not in another country. Angry enough to want to stand on my own two legs. I was brought up to have pride in my country. Call it *esprit de corps*. I love it. It's inside me. It's even a blessing to love my country. Even when it gives me ulcers. And the ulcers will stop the day all the schools get an education before being allowed to open their doors." There was a bubble of sadness in Trent's voice. "All I wanted was an education but they wouldn't let me..."

Trent was sniffling. Johnny had to wait, had to let him get it all out of his system, for five minutes at least, before he asked about Sloan and the murder in the kitchen.

"I can't blame those students," Trent sighed. "They were brought up to hate the color of my skin. It's their blueprint for delinquents, the birth of lynchings, the disease that is carried on to those yet unborn. Those poor sick children are taught to depend on their parent's claws instead of their love." A bitter grunt sounded from his bed. "The irony is that many Negroes are mulatto and integration is well established in Dixie."

The Hole was silent now.

Johnny waited no longer.

"Remember Sloan who was killed in the kitchen with a butcher knife?"

"The first day I went to school a woman held up her child so that he could reach out and beat me with his little fists. I remember Sloan."

Johnny swallowed. "Did you see the doctor who killed him?"

"Wasn't a doctor," Trent snorted. "He was an attendant. I even arranged for private tutors to give me an assist in my grades to take no chances that the university would flunk me."

"Do you know his name?" Johnny insisted.

"Of course. I saw him kill Sloan, didn't I? Did you know my house was attacked by night-riding shotgunners?"

Johnny twisted against the straitjacket. "Will you tell me his name?"

"Sure."

"Please, Trent—" The awful sound in Trent's voice alerted Johnny. It was coming again. That blanket of insanity that shrouded everything.

Trent sat up, his body vibrating.

"Get that nigger!" he shouted. "He's not going to school with *my* daughter!"

"Trent!"

"First the classroom, then the school dances and you know *what* after that. Go home, nigger! Go to your own black school!"

"Trent! Trent!"

"Nigger! Nigger! Nigger!"

The words pounded. Johnny tried to rise, his own brain spinning.

"Trent! Snap out of it! Listen to me—"

"I'm for pure Americanism! White supremacy!"

The Hole closed in on Johnny Barrett. Trapped with a brilliant madman whose mind had turned against every single molecule of his natural spirit.

"Burn that Freedom Bus! Burn those Freedom Riders!"

Johnny Barrett screamed. "Shut up, Trent! For God's sake, shut up!"

Trent was quiet but the damage was done.

Johnny felt himself slipping over the rim into nightmare again.

"What a beautiful child, Mrs. Barrett!"

"Isn't he? We're going to call him John."

A baby in a crib, cooing and gurgling. Then the baby is a boy, standing before another crib in which another infant tosses restlessly.

"Now you have a baby sister, John."

"What's her name, Mommy?"

"Cathy."

"Cathy's a pretty name. I like that."

Johnny Barrett woke up the next morning with another of his violent, splitting headaches. Trent was sleeping soundly.

He didn't tell Cathy about his nightmares when she came to visit him after he got out of The Hole. He hardly looked at Cathy. He didn't see the trouble lines in her face nor the shocked expression of her eyes at the sight of him. He was too wrapped up in the futility of his near-miss with Trent.

"That close!" Johnny held up his thumb and forefinger an inch apart. "I was that close to getting the name of the killer when Trent went nuts again. And now they've got him isolated all over again."

Cathy's pale face said nothing. Her features were drawn. There were more hollows under her beautiful eyes.

"But there's still Boden." Johnny was so grim about everything. "I'll reach him and I won't let him waste even one sane moment. I'll ask him about the murder right away. Cathy! I'm sitting right on top of the story."

"Yes, darling."

He frowned at her, holding his hand out and touching her cheek gently. "Are you all right, Cathy?"

She tried to fool him but she couldn't. She

broke down in front of him. "Oh, Johnny—Johnny!"

She threw her arms about his neck, kissing him hard on the lips. He recoiled, shock washing his face, his right hand mopping furiously at his lips.

"Don't ever kiss me like that!"

Cathy was stunned. *"What?"*

Johnny shifted uncomfortably. "You know what I mean."

The rising panic in Cathy wouldn't stop swelling.

"No, I don't know what you mean. You tell me, Johnny."

He averted his face as if he were afraid that Wilkes, Lloyd or the other patients had seen them kiss. Cathy clutched his arm.

"What do you mean I should never kiss you like that? What is it, Johnny? What's the matter? Talk to me, Johnny!" Cathy was shouting now.

Lloyd loomed at their bench.

"I'm sorry, Miss Barrett. But you're exciting the other patients. Please—"

Cathy refused to take her eyes or her hand off Johnny.

"What do you mean, Johnny? Tell me! Tell me!"

She was still crying hysterically when Lloyd escorted her out of the visitor's room. Johnny Barrett looked incredulously at Wilkes, whose kind face was in evidence again.

"Now what's the matter with *her*?" Johnny asked plaintively.

Swanee got Cathy on the telephone at the club between numbers.

"Yes?" Cathy said, more dead than alive.

"Doc Fong told me you saw Johnny today."

"That was last week."

"But you went to the hospital today, didn't you?"

Cathy's tone was flat. "Dr. Cristo sent for me. I told him I thought Johnny was getting worse. He agreed with me."

Swanee made a noise from his end of the phone.

"Did you tell him the truth?"

"No."

"Why did he send for you?" Swanee's voice was suspicious.

Cathy steeled herself. It was awful to talk about it so matter-of-factly. "To get my permission to give Johnny electric shock treatments."

Swanee's monumental gasp was somehow satisfying, in view of his casual acceptance of the whole plan in the first place.

"Cathy, have you lost your marbles? Johnny can't take that kind of punishment! He'll crack! They'll find out he's a fake!"

"I hope they do," Cathy blurted. "But it won't be me who'll expose him. He'll expose himself."

"You should have refused the electric shock,"

Swanee scolded her. "After all, he knows the killer's an attendant and he's bound to find out his identity from Boden at the rate he's going."

"At the rate he's going," Cathy said dully, "I don't know if he'll know his *own* identity."

"What are you talking about?" Swanee bellowed, alarm in his usually confident voice.

Cathy sobbed quietly into the phone.

"He's beginning to think I'm really his sister."

She didn't wait for his answer. She hung up with a click of sound.

Insanity is a stranger who stalks the corridors of the mind, seeking entrance at one of the many little doors.
Mark Dane, White Legs

THE WALL

DR. CRISTO was rubbing cream into his temples when Johnny realized he was seconds away from electric shock treatment. They had strapped him to the table, naturally. Lloyd, moving quietly and with malicious emphasis, placed two electrodes over Johnny's temporal areas. Solicitous Wilkes then placed a mouth gag into position. Johnny knew what that was for. To prevent injury to the tongue and cheeks.

Cristo tried to look kind about everything but Johnny wasn't fooled. He had heard about electric shock treatments. It wasn't as easy as a dental appointment.

Got to hang on. Can't bust down and let them know why I'm here. That crazy Cathy giving them permission to shock me with electricity. When I come to I've got to hang on. I'll be in another world but I've got to hang on. Got to crack Boden. Got to crack Boden. Got to—

The horrifying sound that emerged from the

cavern of his throat was a deep cry from the subconscious as the electric current passed between the two electrodes.

Johnny Barrett convulsed, still screaming.

His head flew apart in a million pieces.

"How are you feeling today, John?"

Dr. Cristo was waiting for his answer. He tried to open his mouth and no sound came. *What's the matter with my voice? Why can't I talk?*

"What is it, John?" Cristo was leaning over the bed, concern etched in his angular face.

I'll try again. "I'm fine," Johnny blurted.

Cristo's eyes squinted. "Was there something wrong a moment ago?"

"No."

"You're not holding anything back, are you, John?"

"No, sir." *But my throat feels funny.*

"Think another shock treatment will help?" The doctor was smiling.

Johnny grinned. "Not unless you strap me in a chair and pull the switch all the way. I've learned my lesson, Doctor."

"No more race riots in the corridor?"

"A midget could lick me the way I feel."

Cristo studied the chart at the foot of the bed. He tucked a ball pen into his breast pocket, nodding in satisfaction.

"All right, John. You can stretch your legs in The Street during make-friends hour."

Johnny nodded too, hardly able to scream the happiness that churned in his insides. *I beat them all! They didn't learn a thing.*

Only a slight worry marred his elation.

Why did I lose my power of speech—even if only for an instant?

He hardly thought of Cathy.

The Street was the same as usual.

Johnny met up with Pagliacci, Methuselah, Jekyll and Hyde and all the rest, busy with their own dreams. Stuart walked by him, whistling *Dixie*, his face happy and foolish but he gave no sign that he recognized Johnny. Pagliacci was sawing the air with his arms as he boomed: *"Figaro . . . Figaro! Hey, Figaro!"* No, The Street hadn't changed. It was the same mixture as before. The mute, the catatonic, the schizoid, the paranoiac. And Johnny Barrett.

Somehow, the corridor seemed longer than he remembered. He scratched his head, at a loss to understand The Street's new length. Maybe an addition had been made. Maybe they had lengthened it.

He put aside the baffling discovery and searched for Boden. He had to be somewhere in the mass of look-alike greys and whites.

Maybe Boden is dead. I'd have heard about it

though. How could I? Maybe he died while I was in The Hole.

A catatonic laughed out loud as he passed.

Johnny's brows furrowed almost angrily. Then a happy thought replaced it. The story. He'd be syndicated all over the country with a yarn like that. Hollywood paid big money for sensation. He could buy a farm in New England and he and Cathy could get married and raise a flock of kids.

"That's what she always wanted. I miss her so much. I'd give anything to make love to her—

The shabby figure sitting on the floor, back against the wall, hunched over a pad of paper, drawing with a piece of charcoal, made him pull up short in amazement.

Boden!

Johnny paused before him, staring. The man was in his late fifties, yielding to soft fat, his smooth face looking calm and unworried. Loose, wiry blond hair clung to a rounded head.

Dr. Boden. American physicist, Nobel Prize winner, worked on the atom bomb, the H-bomb; a brilliant scientist, went insane working on nuclear fission, missiles, rockets to the moon. Hobby: painting.

The drawing, from what Johnny could see of it, was a house. As a child might draw it. Only the lines had the force and pressure of an adult. Boden's breakdown had left him with the mentality of a six-year-old.

"Hello," Johnny said, as he might to a six-year-old child.

"H'lo," Boden said, not looking up.

"Have you been away?"

Boden nodded, still busy with his sketch. "We played games. Wanna play with me?"

"Uh huh."

The giant intellect on the floor sprang erect eagerly, drawing pad discarded. "Let's play hide-and-seek."

"I like that," Johnny said.

"Hide your face," Boden cautioned. "Count ten."

His heart went out as he closed his hands over his eyes. The scientist had clambered under a bench nearby. His face was happy.

"One, two," Johnny counted, "three, four, five, six, seven, eight, nine, ten—"

Under the bench, Boden was giggling happily, holding his hands to his mouth as Johnny Barrett made a big fuss about not finding him. With his heart breaking, Johnny made sure he lost the game.

It went like that for a week.

During make-friends hour on The Street, Johnny sought out Boden. They played games and Johnny crowed over Boden's drawings. The scientist was delighted with his new friend. Epecially a friend who was willing to pose for picture after picture. A friend who laughed with him and didn't make fun of him the way some of the other fellows did. Johnny could see the appreciation in Boden's eyes.

"Now," Johnny said, at the very height of their new friendship, "you make a real good picture of me so I can hang it on my wall."

Boden made some fast lines on the pad and held the result up, grinning mischievously.

"Aw." Johnny made a face. "You can draw me better than that."

Boden frowned, then bent over his pad, looking up at Johnny with a critic's gaze and drawing more slowly. Johnny kept still, holding a face-front pose. He had to work on Boden carefully. He was different from Stuart and Trent who had begun with suspicion. Boden was simple. Child-simple. You had to be patient with kids.

Wilkes and Lloyd wandered by and looked questioningly at Johnny.

"Helps keep me out of trouble, doesn't it?"

Wilkes nodded. "You know who he is?" He poked a thumb at the busy, miles-away Boden.

"He's my friend," Johnny said.

Wilkes smiled. "What does he talk to you about?"

"Kid games."

Strangely enough, even unfriendly Lloyd liked that.

"Keep it up, John. Maybe *you* can help him. We can't."

They left, leaving Johnny and Boden alone again. As their steps receded, Boden exhibited his second drawing of Johnny. It was still merely a forceful scrawl but there was a slight improvement.

"You know," Johnny said, "if you draw a real good picture of me, I'll show you a new game."

Boden clapped his hands. "Show me the game!"

"After you draw a real good picture of me."

Boden pouted. "No!"

Johnny pouted too. "Then I won't show you the game."

"Ohhh," Boden hesitated, stubbornly, "all right for you."

He picked up the pad again, moistened the charcoal with his tongue and began to sketch slowly. His eyes gleamed childishly.

The visiting room had changed too. Sunlight poured through the wired windows and everything looked pleasant and nice. Johnny's heart raced when Cathy came in. He ran to her, folding her in his arms with all the passionate fervor of the old Johnny. Cathy was so happy at the exuberance of the welcome that she wanted to cry. Johnny shushed her, holding her by the hand and whispering urgently in her ear so that nobody else could hear.

"Honey, I've got Boden making a portrait of me. It's taken weeks but it's a professional portrait. He was a wonderful artist, you know. Einstein's hobby was the fiddle and Boden's is drawing. He's still got the mind of a child, but his hand has the stroke of an adult. Imagine, your Johnny giving therapeutic treatments to Dr. Boden!"

"You look so much better than last time, Johnny."

He chuckled. "Tell Swanee any minute Boden's apt to snap back to sanity. And when that happens I'll crack this jigsaw."

Cathy was still too confused about the change in him to make any sense out of things.

"What about my perjury?"

He kissed her worried mouth.

"Cathy, darling, Dr. Cristo will be grateful. Don't you see? The killer could score another victim if he isn't exposed. The judge will understand why you lied. It's for a cause, Cathy. And what a cause!"

"Johnny."

"Hmmm?"

"Do you still love me? As a woman?"

He grabbed her exultantly, his face burst with a smile. "Is there any other way?"

She couldn't answer him.

The change before her very eyes had planted her solidly on Cloud Nine.

Ward B was roused the next morning by the booming services of Pagliacci. His large voice rolled over the room, stirring Methuselah, Jekyll and Hyde and Unrelieved Melancholy. They groaned awake.

"Breakfast bell. Wake up, John." Pagliacci's mountainous bulk vibrated as he yawned.

Johnny wanted to say good morning back but no sound came. His fingers raced to his throat.

Pagliacci smiled. "Good morning, John."

What's the matter with me? I can't talk!

"Good morning!" It shot out of him so suddenly he blinked at Pagliacci. The giant laughed.

"Don't invade my domain, John. Only opera singers are allowed to lose their voices. Remember Caruso?"

"Good morning," Johnny said again, louder this time.

"That's better, Giovanni. You're playing too much with that artist patient. If you don't watch out, he'll drive you crazy. He's really an amateur psycho—a man with the mind of a child."

Johnny Barrett thought about that all morning until it was time to visit The Street again for the make-friends hour. But he kept on rubbing his throat and testing his vocal cords. Damn, but it was funny. Funny and frightening.

Why does it keep happening?

Boden was ready and waiting as usual.

Johnny sat down on the bench to pose. The portrait was nearly done. The time was near for the great revelation. Maybe another revelation too. But Johnny doubted it. Boden had remained exactly the same in all the time they had spent together.

Johnny never saw the miracle that Boden did, the one that came so suddenly. Only Boden heard the voices. The strange voices that called for Dr. Boden, wanted him at the Pentagon, insisted he report to the Joint Chiefs of Staff.

Johnny was only aware of the change when he saw Boden look to the ceiling as if seeing some strange wonderful sight. The change in the man's face was like black magic. The blank childish expression dissolved into the face of an older, wiser generation.

Boden's pad and charcoal sketch slipped from his fingers. He ignored Johnny.

"Not again!" he snapped in a crisp, authoritative voice. "Rockets were fired off Newfoundland back in '53. We detected the first hint of the radiation belt, didn't we? Let me alone, I'm through!"

He retrieved the pad and charcoal, looked at Johnny keenly, unaware of the surprise he found in that face, and continued with his drawing.

"You know, John," he said mildly, "we are too sophisticated in the art of death. Hold still, John, you're moving around too much."

Johnny was all set to ask about Sloan when he felt the constriction of his throat. He knew he couldn't talk again. His tongue was thick, his vocal cords paralyzed.

"There is a sense of doom and crisis," Boden said. "You're moving again, John."

Please. Let me ask him. I've got to ask him!

"We have too many intellectuals who are afraid to use the pistol of common sense. Afraid of their own lives. And I am one of them, my boy. Hold still, please."

Johnny strained against the wall, sweat beading his forehead. Boden went on sketching.

I'll write the question. No! It's liable to snap him back to childhood. I've got to get my voice back!

"Throughout the world there is a great symphony of total eradication and I helped to compose the movements to stop anything that moves. John—" Boden looked up, annoyed.

"How can I finish this portrait looking at your back?"

Johnny writhed, trying to speak.

Don't panic. It came back in the ward, didn't it? Don't panic!

"I found myself fighting my own mind and reason, my dream destroyed on the battlefield." He checked Johnny's eyes. "Ah, I'm getting it, fine. Yes, my boy, I got fed up with Man taking a daily hammer-and-sickle coated pill of venom."

Johnny swallowed, straining. *Please let me ask him!*

"You see, John, I was brought up with the belief that the first value of worth is the preservation of humanity but instead I found myself constantly faced with the choice of thermonuclear disaster or appeasement with an enemy power that thrives on monstrous propaganda and false preachments. Propaganda and panic. The twin devils poisoning our human condition. I'll be through soon, my boy." He made short strokes on the pad.

No. Keep talking. Keep drawing. Keep talking.

Boden scowled.

"I'm a pure scientist. Let the Russians claim the bigger satellites. If they are the first to discover the mating habits of sea horses, must we race them to discover the inner cellular structure of a grasshopper's brain?"

Johnny sweated, his brain pounding.

Who killed Sloan in the kitchen?

Who killed Sloan in the kitchen?

Who killed Sloan in the kitchen?

If I keep saying the words over and over in

my mind maybe they'll jump out of my mouth!

"John," Boden tsk-tsked. "Please stop moving your mouth. It's very disconcerting." He drew a line on the pad. "There must be a reason why we are here on earth, be it scientific, religious or natural phenomena."

Who killed Sloan in the kitchen?

"And since we don't know the reason we should take advantage of our ignorance and quit living like tigers in bomb shelters replacing homes and poisoned air replacing the free air we were blessed to breathe."

Who killed Sloan in the kitchen?

The charcoal spurted on. "Today everybody is giving the human race two weeks to get out. I cannot live with a two-week notice. And so, I quit living."

"Who killed Sloan in the kitchen?" The blessed words poured out of Johnny Barrett's mouth.

Boden appraised his work. "It's finished, John."

"Who killed Sloan in the kitchen?" Johnny gasped the query again.

"Oh, yes." Boden looked thoughtful. "I remember poor Sloan. Ward C, bed four. For an insane man he had morals. I was in the kitchen with two friends. We were under the table—"

"Who killed him?"

"I can't tell why we were under the table but there we were and we saw Sloan confront this attendant—"

"What's his name?"

"And Sloan threatened to expose him to Dr. Cristo," Boden prattled on, "for taking sexual advantage of feeble-minded women in the ladies' ward."

Johnny was on the verge of collapse. His breathing came hard. "Who?" he whimpered hoarsely.

"Wilkes," Boden said, holding up the drawing, smiling. "Take a look, John. It's a perfect likeness of you."

Wilkes! Wilkes! I've broken the story!

He hardly saw the portrait of himself which Boden was holding up proudly. His head was on fire with triumph. It was only when Boden held it before his face, that he recoiled.

"What's that?" he shuddered.

"Your portrait, of course," Boden said, puzzled.

"You must be crazy," Johnny Barrett said. "That's not me."

It couldn't be.

The face in the portrait was cold and hard. The cheeks drawn and haggard. The eyes wild and unreasoning—with the glassy intensity of the confirmed psychotic.

"I only paint what I see," Boden was saying in a hurt tone of voice. The child in him had very nearly returned with this one rebuff from a friend.

The friend, whose name was John, suddenly screamed hysterically, seized the portrait and tore it to pieces. Before Boden could protect himself, Johnny Barrett had sprung at him, fists pounding, mouthing insane, violent, ugly things.

The Street came alive with the blasting of attendant's whistles.

. . . we kiss in a shadow.
Rodgers and Hammerstein, The King and I

THE OUTSIDE

CATHY stared at her naked body in the dressing room mirror and shivered. The damp sheen left over from the last performance of the evening made her flesh glow strangely. The garish lights of the cluttered room highspotted the tumbling cascade of her long hair. Cathy looked into her own eyes and didn't like what she saw there. She saw a lonely woman with a jungle look. She shuddered again and reached for her orange robe. The one Johnny always liked. Johnny. She tried awfully hard not to remember him.

"Coming, Cathy?"

Nadine, who drove the marks crazy with three advantageously placed balloons, was calling from the doorway. Nadine was a stunning brunette with huge dimensions also advantageously placed.

Cathy drew a comb through her trailing hair, defeat making a cruel cramp of her lush mouth.

"No, thanks, kid. It's home for me from now on."

"Cathy," Nadine said reproachfully.

"Sorry, Nadine. You run along. Have a good time."

Nadine shifted in the doorway. "Just think, kitten. There'll be some good-looking rich slobs at the party and you could forget your troubles in style. I know you and Johnny had a split-up of some kind and you're ape about the guy, but why suffer? Come on—"

"No."

"Okay," Nadine barked, her tone tightening. "It's your life. You mess it up any way you like." The door slammed behind her and Cathy was alone. Always the last girl to go home from the club these days.

The raspy bite of the comb into her blonde hair was unnerving. Cathy dropped the comb among the clutter of the table. The face in the mirror taunted her again. Shadows under the eyes, cheeks getting thin and that damn vein jumping out on the right side of her forehead. Johnny Barrett and his fine schemes. She was in great shape. The way these things went, she was liable to join him in the laughing academy any day now. Johnny, Johnny.

She was all too aware of the taut pull of her firm breasts on her chest wall. And that stirring sensation in the pit of her stomach. Her thighs ached unbearably.

Damn Johnny. Damn Swanee. Damn Doc Fong. And damn the day her man had gotten his fingers on a juicy murder story that seemed to him to be the key to his ambitions and his life's ideals. The Pulitzer Prize. Cathy caught a sob in her throat before it could emerge. Cathy should be the prize that Johnny Barrett wanted. But it wasn't that way, was it? It was never that way with men. They weren't like women; content with home, kids and happiness. No, they had to run out and do things and win things and get promoted. Oh, damn—

She found a cigarette left in the crumpled package near the Kleenex box. It took her seconds to light the thing. She inhaled fervidly, sucking in her abdomen.

It wasn't fair. It just wasn't fair.

Why should she be alone? The fairest of the fair, they said. Why should she be a faithful convent nun for a fool? The best body on the boards, they said. Why should she suffer for a fantastic scheme? The lovely, adorable, desirable Cathy the Singing Stripper?

Swanee and his tangerine. Fong and his pencil. Johnny and his scheme. As for Johnny—

Bitterly, Cathy realized she was crying again, the tears running free down her tired face.

"Cut it out," a man's heavy voice said suddenly behind her.

Cathy raised her head to the mirror. There was no peace left in the world. Not her world, anyway.

Connor was standing behind her, his big shoulders leaning against the dressing room door. His insolent eyes were cold and the thin cigarette jutting from his fleshy lips went well with the sophisticated cut of his dinner jacket and bow tie. The dark sheen of his brushed-back hair and the tan health of his hard-boned face were as polished as ever.

"Even bosses ought to knock," Cathy said huskily. "And mind your own business."

Connor didn't move. He took the cigarette from his lips and shook his head impatiently.

"For the best looking woman I've ever seen, from Maine to Tahiti, you are one large sap, Cathy."

"Thanks for the information," she said coldly. "If you don't mind, I want to get dressed."

"I'll watch."

Cathy swiveled in her chair to face him, tightening her robe over her nakedness.

"I'd hate to tear up my contract, Connor. I like working here in spite of everything."

Connor said. "That's damn good of you. Nothing wrong with five hundred a week, is there?"

She sighed and returned to the mirror.

"What do you really want besides adding me to your collection?"

Connor came forward and loomed in the mirror like a giant.

"I know what's going on, I see my chance and I try again. What's wrong with that?"

Cathy stiffened. "What's going on?"

He shrugged and tried to place his meaty hands on her shoulders. She twisted away and he regarded the tip of his cigarette casually.

"Things get around in a club. The waiters talk, the girls talk, the musicians hear things. And then the boss hears things. One way or another, the truth will out."

"Truth?" Cathy tried hard not to sneer.

"What would a thief like you know about truth?"

Connor laughed. "One of the reasons I go for you, Cathy, is that fine Irish lip of yours. You've got guts talking to me like that. Anybody else would have a broken arm at this point of the conversation."

Cathy controlled her nerves. "So?"

"Scuttlebutt tells me that Johnny Barrett is away. *Permanently* away. I hear he snapped his cap and you've been running up to some nut factory on visitor's day. Is that true?"

"And if it is?"

Connor looked sympathetic. "Well, don't bite my head off. If it's true, I'm sorry. If it's really over, I'm putting my bid in again. Can't have my favorite peeler unhappy."

Cathy sighed. "Okay. It's nice of you to care. Now beat it, will you. I want to get home and get some rest."

"Seeing Johnny tomorrow?"

"Maybe."

"Must be rough. If he's really off his rocker."

"It is."

"Rough," Conner repeated. "But very interesting."

His hand fell to Cathy's shoulder and burned there. She tried to pull away but suddenly his other arm had snaked around her guard.

"Listen, kitten," he said softly, without rushing his words. "Don't mark me off as a slob with no good intentions. I've got it for you. Bad. I've had my share of the girls, as you know. For you I'll wrap it all up and vote the straight Cathy ticket. I don't want to hurt you. Do it my way and we'll be partners forever."

"Connor, you bastard."

"That's it. Tough. I like you tough."

Cathy tried to move away. She couldn't. His other hand began to caress, flexing masterfully.

"Connor—"

"Say the magic word, Cathy, and the world is yours."

Before she could answer, he had jerked the wooden chair back and pulled her up easily into his massive embrace. Cathy's robe parted. She saw the feverish gleam in Connor's eyes, the wide-mouthed sensual approval in the smile of his big mouth. Cathy closed her eyes, her arms suddenly powerless to resist. Connor pressed his rough body into her. His waist slammed her. His thighs anchored her nudity like a suction. The coarse material of his clothes burned her, bruised her.

She moaned and hung onto him. The anger, the hurt and the emptiness of the last two months exploded with the violence of unexpected interruption.

"See, Cathy?" Connor's voice was a throb of wonder. "I'm not so hard to take."

"Connor—" she gasped, unthinking.

"Soon as you forget this Johnny, we'll—"

Johnny. Johnny Barrett. The man I love. The man I want.

The room straightened, the garish lights putting everything back in its proper perspective. The grease paint, the Kleenex, the dirty bulbs, the hanging sequins and G-strings. Her whole body rebelled, revolting against the loss of time and place and reality.

"Let me go, Connor," Cathy said coldly.

His laugh was harsh. "You're kidding!"

"I'll scream if you don't."

"Now you are being funny. Who'll hear you if you do?"

She drew her head back and spat full into his face. She might have lost her head for a minute about who she was and what she was and where she was but she was no hysterical Jane who'd shout, "Rape!" to the nearest policeman. But she felt now that Connor had violated her and the indignity made the spittle fly from her mouth.

It was more effective than fingernails, a slap or a scream.

Connor released his hold and staggered back. Cathy felt behind her on the dressing table for a heavy hair brush. She really didn't know what he would do now.

The flash of crimson in his confident face was like a rainbow of anger. His eyes glinted almost maniacally.

"I ought to fix your face for that," he rasped. "Nobody ever spit on Joe Connor."

Cathy kept her nerve. "It was worth it, wasn't it, Connor? You got closer than you ever got before. Don't complain."

"What the hell is the matter with you?" he roared suddenly, all his masculine exasperation coming to the surface. "You lead me on and now you turn it off. Dames! I should have my head examined."

"I'm hooked body and soul to a boyscout

newspaper reporter who I just can't live without. Now, will you get the hell out of here and leave me alone?"

Connor had not come up the hard way for nothing. He had not slugged out a tough living in a brutal world without knowing a stacked deck when he saw one. He knew how to win but he also knew how to lose.

"Excuse it, Cathy. I'll go."

"Thanks, Connor."

"See you tomorrow?"

"See you tomorrow."

After he had gone, Cathy dressed for the street like a dead woman. Her movements were stiff and lifeless. Like those catatonics with Johnny up at the Mental Hospital. She couldn't help remembering how awful he looked now. The lines on his face and the worry in his eyes. Maybe he was play-acting and all but it was so dangerous playing games like that with your mind. Wasn't it? She didn't care what Doc Fong and Swanee thought. The Bible was right. If you played with fire, you got burned.

Her own act was getting tougher and tougher with each performance. Bumping, grinding, hitting your pelvis into the center field bleachers was a mockery when you did it for strangers night after night. Even the fancy salary didn't change that.

She didn't want dry runs. She wanted Johnny. Why the hell didn't he want her as much as she wanted him?

She locked the dressing room door behind her and walked down the hall out of the club.

The click of her high heels made hollow thumps in her subconscious.

She tried to think of something else beside the disturbing fact that she was seeing Johnny again tomorrow. Seeing and playing the deadly, unnatural game of I'm-his-sister-and-he-tried-to-rape-me-and-isn't-that-terrible?

It was terrible, all right.

Terrible that it didn't have a chance of coming true for a long, long time.

What ho! this fellow is dancing mad.
He hath been bitten by the tarantula.
Edgar Allan Poe, The Gold Bug

THE WINDOW

THE STRAITJACKET brought back memories of The Hole and Trent. It was different this time, though. A quiet white room and total recall of his attack on poor Boden. With one glaring exception. One maddening defect of logic.

Boden gave me the name of the killer. He named the killer and I can't remember that name!

He didn't have time to worry about that, though. Dr. Cristo and Wilkes came to see him. Cristo's lean face was troubled. Wilkes' was as kindly as ever. Johnny felt like a rat for the hard time he was giving them. It was as if their sympathy was misplaced. Or just abused.

"Did I hurt Boden too much?" Johnny asked.

Dr. Cristo shook his head. "He's playing his games on the floor again. He'll be all right."

"I'm glad I didn't hurt him. It's tough being in this straitjacket all night."

"You've been in here for two whole weeks, John."

Two weeks? Where did they go? I thought it happened today. He's lying to me. I'd know if I'd been here two weeks . . . if only I knew the name that Boden gave me! I remember! I remember!

"Dr. Cristo," Johnny said, eyes bright, "I know who killed Sloan in the kitchen."

Cristo and Wilkes matched expressions. Cristo looked sad.

"You've been hearing stories from the patients, John."

"I'm telling you I remember. Call my paper. Call Swanee. Tell him I know. I know the killer. It's Dr. Cristo. No—it's Cathy. No, I killed Sloan. Yes, that's it. I killed Sloan!"

Dr. Cristo wasn't listening. He had turned away to talk to Wilkes. "Keep him under restraint until further orders."

Wilkes' answer came sadly, as usual. "Yes, sir."

Johnny Barrett never heard Dr. Cristo leave. He was lying in a new state of awareness, thankful for having remembered the name of Sloan's killer.

"Are you sure you killed Sloan?"

Wilkes' voice purred softly at his ear. *Good old Wilkes.*

"Sure I'm sure."

"Who was it, Mr. Barrett?"

"It was Cathy. Yes, Cathy killed him."

"Why are you interested in Sloan?"

"Wilkes killed him," Johnny said suddenly.

Wilkes' face was placid. "Who told you I killed him?"

"Dr. Cristo. No." Johnny shook his head. The pain was coming back. "It was Cathy. That's who. She killed him."

Wilkes left after that, locking the door. His footsteps clicked down the hall, going away. Johnny stared wild-eyed at the ceiling, his face a mask of perspiration. Anguish tormented his eyes.

"Somebody do something about my head!" he yelled. "It hurts!"

Why would a nice girl like Cathy kill a stranger like Sloan?

The question was driving Johnny Barrett mad.

The day they took him back to Ward B, he was under mild restraint. This consisted of manacling his hands to a leather harness encircling his own waist. His fellow inmates made no comment. Pagliacci sat on his own bed, smiling and saying nothing, Methuselah remained on the floor, covering his head with the familiar sweater. Jekyll and Hyde played their quiet card game, looking neither to the left nor right. Unrelieved Melancholy was staring at the far wall.

None of the men paid any attention when Dr. Cristo marched in with Wilkes and Lloyd in tow. They came over to Johnny, who was fixed stonily at the window sill.

"How do you feel, John?"

Johnny didn't answer.

"Why aren't you taking a little walk down The Street?"

Johnny turned slowly, raised his shackled hands. "With *these* on?"

"What's wrong with them?"

"It's embarrassing."

"That's a good sign." Cristo beamed approval. "How's your headache?"

"Gone. I lost it in that straitjacket."

Wilkes and Lloyd grunted in unison. Cristo smiled.

"Do you know who I am?"

"Dr. Cristo," Johnny said.

"Know him?" The doctor pointed at Wilkes.

"Mr. Wilkes. And that's Mr. Lloyd. I'm a different man, Doctor."

Dr. Cristo's smile froze. "Who killed Sloan?"

I wish I could remember the name. Watch it, now. This might be a trap. Two attendants here. Could be one of them.

"Who?" Johnny asked.

"Sloan."

"Who's Sloan?"

Dr. Cristo nodded in satisfaction and motioned to the belt. "Remove it," he ordered Wilkes.

Lloyd looked happy about the arrangement, too.

"I think it's time you got a little exercise, John," Cristo suggested. He checked his watch. "Relieve Kellogg in Hydro, Wilkes."

"Yes, sir."

When Wilkes had gone, Cristo eyed Johnny closely.

"Do you miss Cathy?"

Careful now.

"Yes, sir."

"How do you feel about her?"

"Oh, you mean that—that crazy feeling I have for her?"

"Is it a crazy feeling?"

Johnny smiled. "I'm a little mixed-up, Doctor. Couple times in The Hole and that room, I got to realizing it's wrong for me to want her. I mean—well—you know what I mean."

"I think you're making real progress, John. Real progress." Dr. Cristo sounded like a teacher proud of a recalcitrant student who was well on the way to becoming a star pupil.

I will as soon as I remember that name.

"See you later, John," Dr. Cristo said and walked out of Ward B with Lloyd.

Pagliacci was beginning to boom something from *Madame Butterfly* when Johnny Barrett went looking for The Street again.

The corridor was nearly deserted.

Johnny found a bench and sat down. He tried to think. Nothing came. The void of memory loss numbed him. What was the matter with him? Couldn't he think of a simple thing like a name? Especially when that name was the one thing necessary for him to give up his masquerade. The Pulitzer Prize for Journalism was as close as that. As far away as the darkness that shrouded the forgotten name.

He stared down the long corridor. A patient drifted into view, ambled slowly toward him. Johnny blinked. Pagliacci. Now why hadn't he recognized the big man immediately? You couldn't mistake Pagliacci for anyone else. Or could you?

He rubbed his eyes. His brain was really getting affected. *What the hell was that name?*

"Hello, John," Pagliacci said, and sat down beside him.

"Hi, Pagliacci."

"We seem to be alone, John."

"Yeah."

Pagliacci chuckled. "The make-friends hour must be getting unpopular."

With that, Pagliacci folded his arms across his mammoth middle and said no more. Johnny accepted the silence, mutually, and went on thinking. He really didn't feel like talking anyway.

What was that name?

An attendant in white pants. Stuart saw it, Trent saw it and Boden saw it. Boden had even named the man.

Johnny rubbed despairingly at his eyes. They ached strangely, as if something were inside trying to get out. *Yeah. Something all right. That unremembered name.*

The first raindrop made Johnny look up in bewilderment. The broad, grey expanse of the ceiling collided with his eyes. Johnny shook his head, bewildered, and stared at the palm of his hand.

A drop of moisture lay glistening there.

A raindrop.

"Feel that?" Johnny said to Pagliacci.

"What?" the big man mumbled absently.

"It's beginning to rain," Johnny Barrett said positively.

Pagliacci grunted. "I like the rain," he said and closed his eyes again.

Suddenly, a crack of thunder hammered on the walls of the corridor. Johnny shuddered in fear and huddled against Pagliacci. A flash of jagged lightning illuminated the long strip of hallway.

Desperately, Johnny stared down the corridor.

It was empty. His eyes swung to his side. Pagliacci was gone. The echoes of the thunder rolled and murmured through the hall. Johnny jumped to his feet.

The rain was beginning to come down with violence.

Johnny lurched forward, running.

Rain was hammering against his body. Large globs of moisture pelting his face and body. His grey denims were getting drenched. Water ran down his legs and slopped off his shoe tops. Wildly, he looked for a concealing doorway.

The corridor yawned before him, traveling like a vanishing perspective of parallel lines into infinity. Johnny screamed. *Where is everybody? How did I get caught in the rain? Why didn't Pagliacci warn me?*

The doors in the corridor were all locked.

Johnny pounded on the door of Ward B, wrenched on the knob. The door remained closed. So did every other door he frantically tried. And still the rain throbbed down, cascading like some fabulous Niagara to cleanse the only man left in the world. Or to drown him.

Johnny screamed again. His hair was dangling in his eyes, his heart pistoning furiously. The frightening rainstorm howled, whistled and bansheed as veritable sheets of water and wind combined to fill the corridor. Johnny slipped and sprawled headlong, his face sliding on the flooded surface of the floor.

He rose into the teeth of a hurricane gale buffeting toward him as if propelled by a monster fan. The chairs and benches were twisting and turning at crazy-corner angles, rocketing toward him with grating noises of doom.

The driving rain engulfed him, drove him to his knees again.

Thousands of gallons of angry water cascaded over the world of the corridor.

Johnny tried to grasp a wall and hang on. He couldn't. The floodtide of nightmare swept him along with it, his last scream blending terribly with the monster noise of the water and the wind.

He was drowning.

Going down, lost—

It was the end of everything. Maybe, the world.

Johnny Barrett opened his eyes.

Somebody was screaming, the awful sound trailing off into a silly bubble of noise.

The corridor was bright and noisy, crowded

with the inmates at their various stages of activity. Johnny's hands flew to his garments, his face, his hair. Dry. Dry as a bone.

Beside him, Pagliacci snickered.

"That was a sour note, John."

It was only then that Johnny realized he was the one who had screamed. That he was the one who had wandered into nightmare and come forth alive, with no one to ever know or care about the dreadful journey he had taken.

Wilkes. I remember! Wilkes!

The name came back, surrounded with the searchlight of awareness, the floodlight of total recall. He could even see Boden's mouth moving as he sounded the name.

Wilkes! Wilkes! Wilkes!

He was sane now. He was exultant. He had to find Dr. Cristo and tell him before anything else happened to upset things. *Wilkes. Of all people. Wilkes!*

"Stop yelling, John," Pagliacci said. "Dr. Cristo is coming over. You don't have to say his name fifteen times."

Yes. Here was Cristo again, looking annoyed but sensible and protective. The clamor of the corridor could not ruffle this sane man.

"You have something to tell me, John?"

Johnny tried to control his excitement but the words seemed to tumble out of him.

"Please, Dr. Cristo. You've got to listen to me. It's important."

"I'm listening, John."

"You've got to let me out. Call my paper. Call Swanee. He knows why I'm here. Please."

"Now, John." Cristo looked disturbed. "Don't start that again."

Johnny couldn't help himself. Control dissolved with the burst of a string of firecrackers. "Wilkes killed Sloan! I swear it! Get Wilkes! I can prove it!"

"I thought you killed him, John," Cristo said persuasively.

Johnny raged, his temper flaming.

"Damn it, Doctor! I'm not nuts! I'm here for the paper! I'm a plant!"

Dr. Cristo sighed and looked around for an attendant. In a panic, Johnny recognized the gesture.

He'll throw me into The Hole. I know that look. I've got to hang on before I have another nightmare. Got to find Wilkes and beat the truth out of him.

"Now, John," Cristo said. "I think we'd better—"

"Sorry, Doctor," Johnny interjected quickly. "It's gone. You once told me there might be a swift relapse even after I feel better, didn't you?"

"Yes."

"Well, I'm okay now. I just got a hot flash that came and went. I'm my own man again."

The doctor looked relieved. "That's more like it, John. Now forget all about Sloan."

"I'll try. I'll really try."

"Good. Why don't you keep Pagliacci company? Have him sing *La Boheme* for you."

"Yes, sir."

Pagliacci smiled when Johnny sat down next to him again. Then the big man shut his eyes, crossed his arms on his bulky body and entered his own private world again. His lips moved and a gentle crooning issued from his mouth. Johnny wasn't listening. He was deep in thought. It was getting increasingly difficult to carry on a hoax of insanity; having to have inner thoughts that were sane and outside ones that weren't. As for Wilkes—

Wait a minute, Johnny Barrett's brain said, *Cristo sent Wilkes somewhere. Where did he send him? Hydro! Hydrotherapy!*

Pagliacci never saw Johnny Barrett stand up and start for the door at the end of the corridor. Even he might have been surprised by the sudden determined sanity in the eyes of the man who slept across from him in Ward B.

The hydrotherapy room was the end of the trail.

Where the solution to the murder of Sloan waited.

Where the killer of Sloan pretended to be the man interested in the welfare of the mentally sick and deranged.

Where the Pulitzer Prize was waiting. Waiting to be picked up by the man who had dreamed of owning it since the day his voice changed.

Johnny Barrett ran toward the hydrotherapy room, fighting his way through the lost souls that blocked the long corridor.

Wilkes saw him as soon as he burst into the room.

Wilkes looked up from the hydrotherapy tub he was adjusting for an elderly patient, surprise making his face blank. Then he saw Johnny Barrett framed in the doorway and he tried to smile.

The smile didn't come off. He saw the look in Johnny Barrett's eyes. The look of sanity, full comprehension and complete ownership of the truth. For a full second, Wilkes' eyes locked with Johnny's. The six patients sitting in their canvas-covered tubs hardly noticed the duel underway before them. Their minds were remote from the scene; their bodies and intellects yielding to the healing powers of icy water. Wilkes tensed. Johnny Barrett came forward, hands upraised. The sound of sloshing water in a filling tub gurgled, slurped and *splattered.*

"How are you, John?" Wilkes said in an unnatural voice.

"Fine, now. You killed Sloan."

"Now, John—" Wilkes was reaching for a weapon. Johnny hardly saw the gesture, his eyes riveting on the man who held the key to everything for him.

"You're going to confess, Wilkes, or I'm going to kill you."

Wilkes' eyes glassed and a smile tugged his mouth corners. His hand strayed. The looped whistle on a string dangling from his neck was suddenly flying toward his lips.

Half of a piercing blast of alarm had issued from the silvery whistle before Johnny hit him. The force of the blow smashed the thing from Wilkes' mouth and his face twisted in a snarl. Johnny flew at him, arms pumping, raining punches into the exposed face. Going by he hit a tub and the patient within groaned. But there was no time to stop, to think, or to make apologies. Wilkes had come back with a vengeance, his trained body responding to an attack from a dangerous mental case.

The battle was a revolving turntable of violence. Nothing was clear. Johnny wrapped his arms around Wilkes' waist and hung on. Wilkes snarled and tried to butt him. Johnny buried his face in Wilkes' chest, the bowtie scraping his chin. Wilkes cursed.

Their locked, heaving bodies battered into the canvas tubs. The table in the room heaved and tilted dangerously. The patients undergoing therapy started to scream. The thin, reedy quality of their cries was lost on Johnny. He had Wilkes and that was all he wanted.

The attendant brought a knee up suddenly and Johnny doubled in agony. He fell back, gasping. A blur of flashing white filled his eyes. Wilkes was getting away. A door slammed. Breathing hard, Johnny hurtled after the blurred motion, got his hands on it again and hung on. He was hardly conscious of the fact that the fight had moved from the hydrotherapy room into the kitchen. The tremendously long wooden table stuffed with trays, dishes and foodstuffs meant nothing to him. He only saw Wilkes and the end of the long trail. Wilkes who had to be stopped. Wilkes who had to confess.

Wilkes was punching him now. He tasted blood. The taste was all mixed up and confused with the stench of cooked vegetables and boiling hot water. Metallic things glittered off the shelves and walls. Spoons, forks, pots, pans, butcher knives—

Wilkes' bloody face wavered before him. Johnny lashed out. The face vanished. He reached, grabbed handfuls of white shirt. The bowtie was askew like some crazy flag. The table pitched. And Johnny Barrett dragged Wilkes by the heels down the long, cluttered table. Wilkes' body ploughed like the prow of a ship, parting the pile of plates and dishes. The kitchen shivered, rattled with noise. Johnny's heart exulted.

"John, John—" Wilkes' voice bubbled.

"Tell me. Tell me. You killed Sloan—"

"No, John—"

He was using Wilkes' body like a ramrod, stuffing the long cannon of the table. But the table ended, dropping away, and Wilkes was free again, Johnny losing his hold. He ran to reach the attendant. Another knee shot into his groin, more feebly this time. Wilkes swayed, fumbled for the doorway and staggered into the next room. Johnny followed, his mind seething with the nearness of victory; his nostrils full of the arena and blood.

They were in the catatonic ward now, hugging, squeezing, kicking and grappling, oblivious of their whereabouts and spectators. The onlookers stared mutely, vacantly, their eyes unequal to the portent of the life and death struggle going on. Wilkes' voice came low, now. The man was strong. Johnny was inspired. His own strength redoubled with the conviction of burning justice.

Far off, he could hear Pagliacci singing. *"I Pagliacci . . ."*

The babble of voices reached his ears. Through a red haze, he stared down at Wilkes' battered face beneath him. It was only then that he realized he was straddling Wilkes' chest, both hands fastened on the attendant's ears as though he were holding a loving cup.

"I'll pull them off if you don't tell me!"

"John—" Wilkes' voice disappeared in agony.

"Who killed Sloan?"

Someone was laughing hysterically like a hyena. The whimper of mirth grew louder.

"Who killed Sloan?"

"Ahhhhh—" Wilkes' eyes shut like a vise. Johnny exerted terrible pressure, wrenching the ears in his hands counterclockwise. Wilkes groaned horribly. The catatonics ringed the men on the floor now and Pagliacci's booming basso profundo pierced the silence. *"Il nome! Il nome!"*

Through the roar, Johnny yelled.

"Who killed Sloan?"

"Ahhhhgggggggrr—" A dying wail escaped the man beneath him.

"Who killed Sloan? Tell me or I'll rip your ears off!"

Pagliacci's voice soared to the ceiling. *"La commedia e finita!"*

The ears in Johnny's hands reddened, burst with color. Wilkes' face was a mask of horror.

"Tell me! Tell me!"

There was no recourse. No mercy. The catatonics surrounding Johnny, spearheaded by the malevolently beaming Pagliacci, were faces from hell.

"I killed him," Wilkes thundered with his last strength, wanting desperately to be heard. *"I killed Sloan!"*

Johnny released his grip on the ears, sitting back on his haunches, with Wilkes' body still pinned beneath him. The red curtain before his eyes lowered. His head felt as light as air. The tremendous weight of tension flew off his shoulders. He took on wings. The corridor was ablaze with light.

And there was Dr. Cristo. And Lloyd.

And Pagliacci.

And the catatonics. And Wilkes lying moaning on the dirty floor.

They were all staring at him, the others. Dr. Cristo's eyes were dumfounded. And Johnny knew he had heard Wilkes' confession. And Lloyd had heard. Everybody had heard.

The singing in Johnny Barrett's blood was a leaping, exhilarating torrent of joy. The flames licked at his body. He was on fire with the paen of conquest hammering in his head.

"John," Dr. Cristo said, "how did you find out about Wilkes?"

"I got myself committed to get that story, Doc." How beautiful the words rolled and rippled on his tongue. "Talk to Stuart, talk to Trent and Boden. They'll tell you what they saw in the kitchen if you get them in a lucid moment."

"Yes, John. Go on."

"Check with the women here. Wilkes molested them, Sloan saw him, and was going to tell you. So Wilkes killed him."

Pagliacci's voice had fallen to a powerful hum that filled the corridor. Lloyd was attending to the fallen Wilkes, his normally hard face softened by comprehension.

"We will, John. Everything as you say." Dr. Cristo was considerably disturbed by the revelation of Wilkes' crime.

Johnny rubbed at his eyes. "And now, if you don't mind, will you call my paper and ask Swanee to confirm that I'm a plant here?" He winked at Dr. Cristo. "I was beginning to feel like I found a home here. You know what I mean?"

Cristo smiled. "I know."

"Well," Johnny Barrett said, wiping the blood from his mouth, "that's a load off my mind."

Ward B was hard to say goodbye to.

There was Pagliacci, Methuselah, Jekyll and Hyde and Unrelieved Melancholy to make farewells to. Johnny couldn't look at them now without feeling a little emotional about it. After all, they were human beings and even though he had been play-acting, he had shared the darkness and the nightmares with them all. The Street he would miss too. That island strip of grey corridor floating in the very middle of this vast hospital.

And then he thought of the story to be written and the prize to be won. And Cathy. Cathy who had waited, who had longed—he throbbed with expectancy. Now, he was eager to be gone.

"Goodbye, Pagliacci."

"Goodbye, Giovanni. Send me some programs from the Met."

"I will. I promise you."

They shook hands, the big man's bear paw a crushing mass of fingers and wide palm.

Methuselah huddled under his sweater, saying nothing. Johnny patted the old shoulder affectionately. Jekyll and Hyde nodded in unison and Unrelieved Melancholy raised a mournful, dog-sad face at his exit.

Johnny Barrett left Ward B, his mind closing a door on the past three months, his intellect embracing the wonderful yarn his typing fingers reportorially ached for.

The corridor stretched before him. The long corridor. The Street where so many broken, unfulfilled longings piled like unseen ghosts in the atmosphere.

He saw Stuart, busy at a bench with some new plan for Gettysburg, his eyes far away from Communism, the bigoted parents, the shock treatments of the present. He did not say goodbye to Stuart. The childish insanity of Stuart was unbearable.

He saw Trent, the dark, black face of mockery beneath the still white placard that said: INTEGRATION AND DEMOCRACY DON'T MIX. GO HOME, NIGGER. Trent was wildly exhorting, his arms windmilling, his eyes blazing. The taunt was ready to spring from his lips; the command poised for utterance. "Grab that nigger before he marries my daughter." He did not say goodbye to Trent. The reverse insanity of Trent was unbearable.

He saw Boden, hunched over his drawing pad, sketching away, his legs crossed like a Hindu beneath him. The strong adult face robbed of intelligence by the mental condition was as naive as a child's. Even the keen eyes were child-keen, mischievous. He did not say goodbye to Boden. The blasphemous insanity of Boden was unbearable.

Johnny Barrett hurried down the long corridor.

He knew what he wanted to do. Story be damned—for now.

Right now, he wanted more than anything else to say hello to Cathy.

A long hello.

. . . so I say to my pal I says let's quit this guy he's nuts!
Robert Riskind, Mr. Deeds Goes to Town

THE WAITING ROOM

SWANEE went to see Dr. Fong in his pleasant offices the day after his disturbing talk with Cathy. Swanee was visibly troubled. Years of being head man of a thriving newspaper had taught him the worth of maintaining a poker face and hiding his tender side but Johnny Barrett had changed things. Swanee didn't feel like peeling a tangerine or being big city bluff or Broadway tough. He loved Johnny Barrett. He didn't want anything to happen to him. Story or no story.

Fong was glad to see him, as always, but he was concerned about the unhappy expression on Swanee's face.

"Cheer yourself up," Fong said coolly. "Visit your friendly Oriental psychiatrist."

Swanee frowned. "No, Doc. No jokes or fast talk. I'm damn worried now."

Fong folded his fingers into a pyramid. He

knew trouble talk when he heard it. "Let's have it, Swanee."

In short, terse sentences not unmixed with the plain language of worry, Swanee related Cathy's belief. The terrifying one that Johnny Barrett was beginning to really think of her as his sister. Fong's eyes clouded momentarily.

"Well," Swanee barked. "Level with me, Doc."

"I see," Fong said thoughtfully.

"I wish I did," Swanee growled impatiently. "I sent a swell kid, a smart newspaperman in on a dangerous assignment. I knew the risks. He did too. But Christ—if he's going to come out of this a loser, no story is worth the price."

"Steady, Swanee."

"I'm sorry, Doc. Cathy threw me for a loss with her report. Oh, I know she's a female and females can get pretty damn emotional but I want to hear it from you."

"Hear what?"

Swanee eyed him carefully.

"Is Johnny going to get burned playing with this fire we started?"

"What do you think, Swanee?"

Swanee spread his arms helplessly.

"I don't want to think. I don't want to guess. Well, tell me, Doc."

Fong swiveled in his chair and un-Orientalized himself to the degree of tugging on his right ear lobe. His wide mouth was a grim, unhappy line.

"I have several degrees, as you know, Swanee. I've spent a good deal of my life trying to understand the human mind. And with all of that knowledge and all the case histories to go by, I am only certain of one thing."

"What's that?"

"The uncertainties." In the stillness of the pleasant office, Swanee blinked.

"Doc, you're telling me it *could* happen. What Cathy said—"

"Yes I am," Fong said sadly. "I know Johnny Barrett. I know he's good and strong and intelligent. But how he reacts to this game he's playing—this pretending to be insane—is something there is no blueprint for. Yes, I *think* he can go the distance. Find his man and come out whole again. But I don't *know* that for a fact."

Swanee rumbled disgustedly. "You say the only certainties are the uncertainties?"

"Where the human mind is concerned, in a word, yes."

"Then maybe we ought to pull him out now while the pulling is good. To hell with the story."

"That's up to you as a newspaperman, of course. As his friend, you know it's just as dangerous for Johnny to withdraw now without accomplishing what he set out to do. His mind would never let him rest if he failed. Remember what I told you."

"Damn me," Swanee shouted. "I never should have let him start this in the first place."

Fong shook his head.

"Too late for that kind of thinking now, Swanee. Much too late."

"So what do we do?"

"Nothing," Dr. Fong said, "but wait, hope and pray."

Swanee cursed bitterly, his big fingers aching for something to peel, strip or smash.

It was as if the room contained a hidden time bomb that he knew was going to explode. But when, where or how and with what effect, he was powerless to say.

"Take it easy, Swanee," Fong said very carefully. "He's my friend, too."

"I know, Doc. But taking it easy is always easier said than done, isn't it?"

As a practicing psychiatrist, Dr. Fong had to silently admit to himself that that was eminently correct. *It's all in your head* had driven more people to doctors than any physical injury.

It was too soon for Headquarters to have received any notification of the events at State Medical Hospital. The sensational capture of a hidden killer might have given Lieutenant Kane, who had signed Johnny Barrett on the books honoring Cathy's complaint, a few fine fits of anger. Kane was a good cop but he didn't go in for crystal ball gazing.

Headquarters always kept him far too busy to imagine things. It was the lot of policemen to take care of first things first.

Like telephones that kept on ringing.

VIPs, cranks, relatives and friends always seemed to want him at the busiest possible times.

And this last one was Old Faithful, the dizzy old dame who wanted to save the world.

Lieutenant Kane was on the telephone, calming down a hysterical woman, when his subordinate, Lennon, walked in, with an expectant air on his face. Kane murmured something into the phone, with smooth instructions, and rung off.

"Busy?" Lennon asked.

"No. Just some woman worried about the bomb again. She calls once a week to warn me. The world is coming to an end."

Lennon shook his head. "Cranks, loonies and phonies. Some life we lead."

Kane made no comment. "You had something for me, Bill?"

"Yeah. Remember that John Barrett? The

newspaperman turned in by his sister. Incest rap."

Kane thought a second. Yes, he remembered. Tall, beautiful female with long blonde hair. A stripper. Barrett was her brother.

"So. What of it?"

"Well, I checked out a few things in the morgue file. That dame *isn't* Barrett's sister."

"What?"

"She just isn't, that's all. I went down to the club where she works and she and this Barrett were engaged to be married. That sound like brother and sister to you?"

Kane looked cynical. "Well, he's crazy. State and County Hospital says he is so there can't be anything fishy about the case."

Lennon looked surprised. "Nothing fishy? She said she was his sister, didn't she?"

"Maybe she was humoring him because he was crazy."

"Maybe she railroaded a hot boy friend she didn't want," Lennon offered.

Kane smiled. "Lennon, when you've been around a little longer, you'll realize a few truths. We didn't angle this one. This dame reported a guy bothering her. She made a complaint. We followed up. So maybe the facts aren't all straight. But the guy turned out to be crazy. That has to be good enough for us. Anyway, that took care of our end of it."

"Aren't you the least bit curious?"

"Curious?" Kane echoed. "Sure I'm curious. But what the hell do you want me to do about it? Check everything down to the last detail? I told you—justice has been served. One annoying maniac was taken off one frightened dame's back. End of quote. End of case."

Lennon looked dour. "Thought I had something. Well, shows to go you."

"Look, boy," Kane said kindly. "I appreciate the effort. Believe me. But don't waste your time with ideas like that. Ask me next time, huh?"

"Okay, Lieutenant." Lennon scratched his nose. "State Mental Hospital, huh?"

"What about *that*?"

"Wasn't that the place where that loony was knifed last year? The one in the kitchen. One of the other loonies did the job—"

"Lennon," Kane said icily, "don't put yourself in a class with the nice old lady who calls me up about the bomb. There just isn't anything in it. Forget it, will you or do you want me to find some work for you to do?"

"I'm going," Lennon laughed, moving nimbly toward the door.

"Don't get so many ideas."

"I had a few about that Cathy dame. You should see the shape she shows off for the customers."

"I can imagine," Lieutenant Kane said drily.

Lennon closed the door behind him, almost gingerly.

The lieutenant poked his thumbs into his eyes and gouged. What a day. Crazy old lady, fast-moving Lennon trying to get a promotion in a big hurry and details, details, details.

But the damage had been done.

Lieutenant Kane, in spite of his best attempts to do otherwise, spent an hour rereading the

John Barrett report. For good measure, he unearthed the Sloan murder from the file. He spent a busy time poring over all the testimony and details. When he was finished, he put both folders back in the file drawer.

He was satisfied. The Department had been served. Done its best and come up with a logical solution each time. Somehow, it was the only possible solution, considering the facts.

Still, it was an odd one, if Lennon was right. Why should a dame say a man was her brother, when he wasn't? That wasn't kosher at all. Not even very nice.

Kane stored the information in the back of his head and went to the pile of business stacked on the top of his cluttered desk. Lieutenant, hah.

Sometimes he felt like a file clerk.

. . . and this was very strange you see, for they hadn't any feet!
Lewis Carroll, Alice in Wonderland

THE EXIT

"HE WAS SANE enough to write the story," Cathy said furiously. "He's been sane for weeks! Don't stand there and tell me you can't do anything for him. Why is he like *that*?"

The shadows under her eyes had deepened. The lush red of her lips had faded. The terror in her eyes was bewildered. Her long, loose hair hung defeatedly.

Johnny Barrett sat in one corner of the office, stationed like an unwinking Buddha on the leather couch under the diplomas and pictures of Freud, Adler and Jung. Johnny was rigid and silent.

Dr. Cristo, from the barrier of his desk, shook his lean head.

"I can't do anything for him *now*. It'll take time."

"Oh, God in heaven!" It was a cry of despair, ripped from her soul.

"Miss Barrett—I'm sorry, Cathy—a man

can't tamper with the mind, live in a mental hospital, subject himself to all kinds of tests—and expect to come out of it sane."

"Doctor, please. What are you saying?"

"John is a catatonic schizophrenic." There was a pause in Cristo's voice as he stared across the room at Johnny Barrett. Johnny, unmoving, unseeing, stared back. "What a tragedy. An insane mute will win the Pulitzer Prize."

"He's not insane!"

The indigation in her eyes burned into Cristo's. He nodded, almost to himself, and raised his voice one level: "John, hold out your hand."

Horrified, Cathy watched.

On command, the mute compliance went into effect with robotlike docility. Johnny Barrett raised his arm, held it out. He kept the arm extended, no expression whatsoever visible on his face.

Cathy shrank into her chair.

"You see? Mute. Catatonic. And he will not put that arm down until he is told to."

"Johnny, Johnny."

"I'm sorry, Cathy."

Her head came up. Her eyes dilated. "Johnny!" she screamed again.

Johnny Barrett never saw her rush to his side, sink before him and engulf him with her arms. Crying, she lifted his other arm and placed them both about her neck. She forced them to encircle her, sobbing bitterly. She held him close, crying his name over and over again, kissing him on the face and lips with feverish rapidity. But there was no response from the dry-eyed robot before her. Love cannot conquer insanity.

Dr. Cristo thought about the truth of that axiom ruefully as he sat, watching Cathy try to heal Johnny Barrett with her heart and soul. The long, loose hair trailed. The robot sat, mechanical and unreal. Cristo emitted a low sigh and stared at the portraits of Freud, Adler and Jung.

"Johnny, Johnny—"

Cathy's wailing, prayerful voice echoed in the stillness of the office of Dr. Cristo.

Miles away, in the office of the *Daily Globe*, Swanee got roaring, boisteringly drunk on a bottle of Scotch, for the first time in his editorial career. The big, gruff man was helpless. What could he do for Johnny Barrett—if he couldn't give him back his mind?

Dr. Fong, not so inscrutable nor Oriental, pored manfully over every book in his reference library at home. There must be something you could do for a friend. There had to be. Else, the whole field of psychoanalysis was a joke.

For Cathy, who had mourned the whole scheme from the beginning, God had looked down, laughed, and slapped Johnny Barrett in the face, for daring to tamper with the formula of life.

"Johnny," she moaned, staring into the dead eyes, "don't you know me? It's Cathy, Johnny. Cathy who wants you, needs you—"

The arms ringed about her neck were stiff and unresponsive.

Johnny Barrett was dead.

Long live the mute catatonic.

The Street was thriving. The make-friends hour always got results. The many benches were crowded; the inmates were talking and idling. The silent ones, wrapped in their solitary cosmos, looked on, unheeding.

Lloyd the attendant had brought a new patient in.

A tall, thin young man who was strangely new and different in this setting. It was evident in his not-yet pale face, his combed hair.

"You came at the make-friends hour, Bob," Lloyd said. "Patients who behave are permitted to congregate in this corridor. They call it 'The Street.' "

"The Street?" Bob echoed.

"Yeah," Lloyd laughed brightly. "A place to gather, make friends, shoot the breeze. You know. You'll like it. You'll see."

Bob followed Lloyd dutifuly down The Street, drinking in the sights new to his unschooled eyes.

He saw tragic faces, smiling faces, expressionless faces, curious faces. The mass greys of the corridor filled the eye as far as it could see. The long strip of hallway seemed to run into nowhere, swallowed up by infinity.

One of the faces they passed belonged to Johnny Barrett.

Trent marched past Johnny Barrett, damning placard aloft, his full-throated voice bellowing, "I believe in white supremacy. America for Americans! Spit in the eye of every black boy you see. Burn him with flaming gasoline, set him on fire with torches! So they like hot music, do they? Then, we'll make it hot for them—"

Pagliacci stood erect, long arms spread in crucifixion. The forgotten arias of his memories poured forth from his deep throat. The notes cannonaded from his subconsciousness.

Stuart frowned over a dog-eared map of Gettysburg, his brows knit in concentration, his youthful face awash with contempt. "Damn you, General Forrest, sir, we can't fall back without losing five thousand men. May I respectfully suggest—"

Methuselah crouched under the cover of his sweater, the world dark around him. Jekyll and Hyde played their silent card game, their twin-like faces rapt and absorbed in the play. Unrelieved Melancholy was crying softly into the folded pyramid of his bony knees.

Boden was crumpling a sheet of drawing paper in despair. He had forgotten his charcoal and couldn't remember where he left it.

The ancient Negro, who was periodically the target of Trent's insanity, huddled terrified beneath his bench as Trent stamped by, looking for him. "Where's that nigger who wants to marry my daughter?"

The long corridor crawled with the chaos of the human mind. The floor writhed with the snakes of nightmare.

Johnny Barrett stirred and looked at the palm of his hand.

A raindrop twinkled like a jewel there.

It was beginning to rain again.

"Cathy, I suggest you don't come back here for a while. It doesn't do any good."

"Please, Dr. Cristo. It helps me to see him. To know at least that he's still alive."

"You know this isn't doing you any good. Hypersensitivity to a loved one's condition is the first step to—"

Cathy clutched the end of the desk with both hands. Her bosom heaved, the woman in her out of control. She spoke and Cristo could hear the effort that went into making that voice steady and normal.

"Doctor, I don't care. I want to see Johnny. I must. Don't spout Freud at me again. I'm sick to hell of Freud."

"All right. As you say. But think over what I said. Stay away—at least till we've made some progress."

"Don't kid me, Doc," Cathy laughed harshly. "You don't ever expect to make Johnny well, do you?"

Dr. Cristo didn't answer her. He rose from his chair and motioned her toward the door. Cathy opened her purse, fumbled for a lipstick and then halted the gesture in defeat.

Why did she have to worry about her face?

Johnny couldn't see it. He wouldn't care if he could. Johnny Barrett couldn't see or care about anything.

She was dry-eyed and stiff as she followed Dr. Cristo out of the office. To The Street. The Street. She could find her way there blindfolded now.

Cathy, the singing Stripper, was an automaton herself as her heels clicked hollowly on the hard floor.

They couldn't have picked a worse time to visit Johnny Barrett.

He was in the very throes of his nightmare.

Sitting on the bench, head flung back, features contorted in a mask of sweaty dread, screaming his head off. Nobody was paying any attention to him. Not even the attendants. The hum of noise peculiar to the street underscored Johnny's screams.

Cathy tried to close her eyes but she couldn't. She might have fallen if Dr. Cristo hadn't suddenly flung out an arm.

The corridor wavered, shimmered and righted itself again.

Cathy's eyes were pulled magnetically to the gallery of the hallway. Where the Still Lifes clashed with the Action Pictures. The ghastly gallery of grey ghosts fluttering, dancing, babbling insanely under the ceiling strip of light that seemed to run into infinity.

The Street was back in business.

The long corridor that stretched into nowhere.

Cathy didn't see Johnny's rainstorm. But she knew it was there.

He said it was.

"Tell me about the rabbits, George."
John Steinbeck Of Mice And Men

THE KEY

"CATHY, the only way to help John is to learn more about him. Through you. You understand that, don't you?" Dr. Cristo's patient voice was like so many tiny pebbles gently disturbing a pool of water.

She sat before him, a Zombi. A beautiful, forlorn Zombi.

"Yes, Doctor. I understand."

"Fine. Now, try and remember–did John ever fondle your hair? I mean–did he ever touch them as if their softness and length excited him?"

She stared at him, his meaning foreign. "Them?"

"Your braids."

"I never had braids." Her tone rose, alien in the quiet of the office. Dr. Cristo's eyes never left her face.

"Think, now. Was there ever a time when John caressed your hair, kissed it with deep emotion? There may be a key in that action, going back to his childhood—"

She flung back her head so that her long golden hair was a waterfall of beauty.

"So he loved my hair. What's that a key to?"

Doc Fong. Dr. Menkin. Dr. Cristo. All those questions, rehearsed at first, and then so tragically real for Johnny. And now the same questions again, for her.

"The key," Cathy repeated dully.

Beyond Dr. Cristo's door, the corridor waited.

blue murder

If you have enjoyed this book, look out for these other superb titles in the Blue Murder series:

WHATEVER HAPPENED TO BABY JANE?
HENRY FARRELL

The book that inspired Robert Aldrich's classic movie, starring Bette Davis and Joan Crawford. "True Grand Guignol, exquisitely calibrated." (*New York Herald Tribune*.)

ISBN 1-85480-032-9

THE BIG CLOCK KENNETH FEARING

"Narrated with force and speed and wit by several voices, it has lasting value as a record of metropolitan life, both inner and outer. In the years since it was written, its clean, brilliant style has shown no sign of fading. Its suspense still catches continually at the throat, and its jokes are still funny." (Ross MacDonald.)

ISBN 1-85480-042-6

SOLOMON'S VINEYARD JONATHAN LATIMER

Banned in America until the 1980s, this vivid portrayal of murder, violence and perverse sexuality is here published in its unexpurgated form. "A genuine hard-boiled classic . . . deserves to be ranked with the best. (*1001 Midnights*.)

ISBN 1-85480-076-0

SOMEBODY'S DONE FOR   DAVID GOODIS

A rare and compelling crime novel by the author of *Shoot the Pianist*, "one of the most satisfying and original post-war hardboiled writers."

ISBN 1-85480-037-X

THE HONEYMOON KILLERS   PAUL BUCK

The novel of the ultimate midnight cult movie, based on the staggering *true* story of Raymond Fernandez and Martha Beck, the bizarre lovers who killed and killed, now published in a revised, expanded edition.

ISBN 1-85480-038-8

TEXAS BY THE TAIL   JIM THOMPSON

First UK publication for this hard-to-find classic by "the best suspense writer going, bar none" (*New York Sunday Times*). The place is Texas, the sun is high in the sky, *anything* can happen. And it does.

ISBN 1-85480-087-6

SCARFACE   ARMITAGE TRAIL

The *first* gangster novel, which inspired the classic gangster film and single-handedly sparked into being an entire genre, *Scarface* is truly a forgotten classic, now back in print for the first time in 50 years.

ISBN 1-85480-053-1